RISE OF DOCTOR FROWNYFACE

The Erotic Sci-Fi Horror Thriller By Dusty Trice

A summer of sex, drugs, and partying by a group of horny young friends ends before it begins when a mad scientist blackmails a perverted mayor while using a biker gang to addict a small town to zombifying drugs, before unleashing a super-virus that causes people to puke themselves to death in order to sell masks and hand sanitizers.

Follow Molly, the mayor's step-daughter, and Holtie, the bad boy from the good side of town, as they fall in love, battle a mad scientist, DOCTOR FROWNYFACE, and try to rescue the world from his sinister clutches. Mad Scientist? He isn't mad. He's just mildly disappointed.

This lyrical satire of a pulp novelization of a B-movie is presented in Read-O-Vision! Now, put on your 3D glasses and enjoy RISE OF DOCTOR FROWNYFACE!

WARNING: SEX! DRUGS! VIOLENCE! FORCED ABORTIONS! BIKER GANGS! A DEADLY SUPER-VIRUS! TRANSVESTITE PROSTITUTES! SPACE ROBBERY! RIVER SHARKS! TOTAL NUCLEAR ANNIHILATION! ADULT CONTENT! 18+ ONLY!

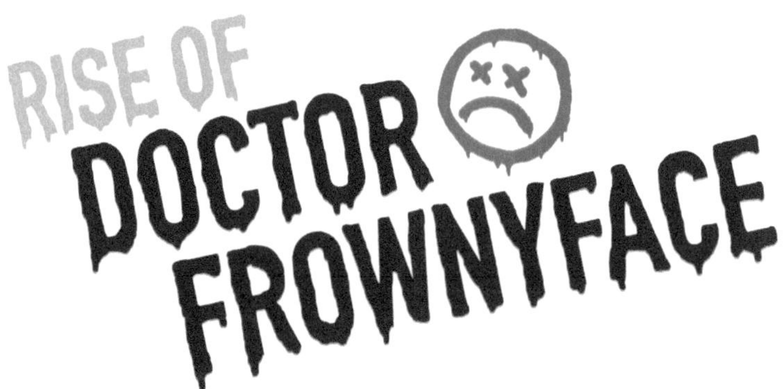

by Dusty Trice

Based on the screenplay by Dusty Trice and Dr. Brian King
Based on an original story and characters by Dusty Trice

ISBN Hardcover: 979-8-9850737-1-3
ISBN Paperback: 979-8-9850737-2-0
ISBN Ebook: 979-8-9850737-0-6

Library of Congress Control Number: 2021920882

First paperback edition December 14, 2021.

Cover Art Design© 2021 Dusty Trice
Cover Art Layout by Dusty Trice
Mayor Photographs© 2021 Sarah Bollinger
Bikini Model Photographs© 2021 Dr. Brian King
Additional Photographs© 2021 Dusty Trice
Pen15 Tattoo Image© 2021 Jovanna Reyes
Additional Images© 2021 Dusty Trice
Book Layout by www.fiverr.com/sarco2000 and
Janie Trice

Read-O-Vision, A Publishing Company
6450 Sunset Blvd. #1107, Hollywood, CA 90028
ReadOVision.com

RISE OF DOCTOR FROWNYFACE

⊗ WARNING

Shut this book immediately. Do not read another word. Stop. I beg you.

What follows is a disgusting and explicit satire and you want no part in it. RISE OF DOCTOR FROWNYFACE is a pulp novelization of a B-movie. The writing is bad, somewhat purposely, of course, but that does not even begin to explain away the perverted horrors and twisted themes contained in this book.

Specifically, if you are my mother, my sister, my grandmother, my aunts and uncles, my cousins, or any of their friends, spouses, coworkers, or children, do NOT read this book. If you are my wife, my father-in-law, any of my wife's siblings, their kids, her cousins, aunts, and uncles, or any of their friends, spouses, or coworkers, go no further. Please, do not come up to me later at a family gathering and say you read this book and you hated it and now you hate me. I did warn you, after all, and I can't thank you enough for NOT reading this book. Thank you.

I will be offering no apologies for this book. If you read it, after I warned you not to, that is your problem. Please don't give me shitty reviews because you read a book you were explicitly told not to read, by the author no less. If you didn't want to deal with controversial thinking, then why did you go start putting ideas in your head. It would save us all a lot of trouble if you just skipped this one and stuck to safer titles with which you agreed. Find a nice Patterson, Rowling, or Grisham, and let us part ways now, still as friends.

A few additional warnings: Do not read this book in public. Do not read this book out loud. Do not read this book at work, at school, or within 50 feet of a church. Do not swim for 30 minutes after reading this book. If you read this book and later decide to burn it, do not stand too close to the fire as the fumes may be toxic. This is especially true if you're burning your ebook reader.

Okay, I think that should do it. You've been properly warned now. I hope to see you again soon when I write something less, uh, trashy. Until next time!

Love,
Dusty Trice

P.S. Do it. Read the book.
You know you want to do it. Do it.

PROLOGUE

The rocket ship hurtled toward the edges of space with its cargo of three billionaire astronauts and a madman. The fully automated space capsule sat perched atop the massive FUCU-2 rocket. The flight was scheduled to be the farthest, and therefore longest, commercial space flight in history.

Dick Memphis, billionaire of the adventurer class, sat strapped to his seat as the rocket propelled the craft skyward. A former record executive, Dick enjoyed parasailing and throwing wild orgies at his private compound on Lemur Island. Dick looked out the windows as the clouds whizzed by and then around the capsule at his "crew" mates, who each clutched a satchel of belongings they could spend the rest of their lives telling people had been to space.

Zif Banjos, the owner of the spacecraft, sat to his right wearing an obnoxious cowboy hat. A prolific online seller of used books, he had made his first billion crushing small businesses by peddling cheap Chinese knockoffs at rock bottom prices from a massive network of overworked and underpaid warehouses.

To Dick's left sat Allen Nosk, the South African gemstone heir and automotive investor, responsible for tunneling beneath earthquake-prone Los Angeles and marketing flamethrowers to nerdy virgin basement dwellers. Nosk made a puckered up duckface back at Memphis in an attempt to look cool.

Directly across from him sat a bald, bearded man in a lab coat and thick black goggles. The man wore a fake mustache, and a monocle stuck to one of the lenses of his goggles with a piece of tape. He also wore a backpack. The man had not introduced himself at the launch site back on Earth, and Memphis had simply assumed this ticketed passenger was perhaps one of Zif Banjos' more eccentric investors. The disguised man in the lab coat gazed back at Memphis with a curious look and a rotten, yellow smile.

"Hello," said the man. "I'm a billionaire."

Something about the stranger didn't sit quite right with Memphis, but all was forgotten as the space capsule reached the peak of its ascent at just over 62 miles above sea level.

"Welcome to the fun zone, gentlemen!" cheered Zif Banjos, as he unbuckled from his seat and floated weightlessly across the cabin. "Who wants to catch some Skittles?"

Memphis opened his satchel and pulled out a 45 vinyl single of the hit song that had launched his empire, Boobular Doobs, a one-hit wonder from a horror movie soundtrack of a bygone era. He spun the record in zero-g and a smile cracked his wrinkled face.

Banjos launched colorful candies across the cabin to Allen Nosk, who floated upside down and caught them in his mouth. Nosk pulled a ping pong ball from his sack and spun it toward the floor. Banjos tossed a handful of candy towards the smiling man in the lab coat. The candy ricocheted off his black goggles and face and floated freely around the capsule.

The man in the lab coat pulled a helmet from his backpack and put it over his head. Zif Banjos was the first of the billionaires to notice the blinking device the man placed on the hatch of the spacecraft.

"Hey! What do you think you're doing?" cried Banjos.

"Give me all your wallets," said the man in the lab coat, as he pulled a gun from his satchel and pointed it at each of the billionaires. Nosk and Memphis froze where they floated at the top of the capsule.

"Are you daft, man? Why would any of us bring our wallets to space?" said Memphis.

Zif Banjos pulled out his wallet and nervously tossed it to the grinning man in the lab coat, who put it in his satchel.

"I've got this covered! Hoohah! Look out now!" yelled Allen Nosk, who kicked off the wall and threw handfuls of ping pong balls that bounced off the man's helmet and clacked erratically against the windows.

"Stop it," said the man in the lab coat. "Empty your pockets and give me your satchels. What about jewelry? Give me your jewelry."

"I don't have any jewelry," Nosk lied. "Are you crazy?"

"Me? Crazy?" cackled the man in the lab coat. "You're the one who has butt hairs growing out of the top of his head."

"That's my natural hairline," huffed Nosk indignantly.

Zif Banjos snorted at Nosk's statement as the man in the lab coat snatched their satchels.

"Why are you laughing?" Nosk snapped at Banjos. "You were a balding pencil-neck fifteen years ago!"

"And now I'm a fucking astronaut, so fuck you!" spat Banjos.

"Gentlemen!" shouted Dick Memphis as he turned to address the man in the lab coat. "Sir, what makes you think you can get away with this?"

"Empty your pockets," the man said as he waved the gun around in the air. "Quickly."

"I have a few emeralds," said Nosk, who handed a fistful of gemstones over. "Do you take bitcoin?"

The man scooped the shiny rocks out of the air with his satchel and produced a small pen-like device with a red button from his pocket.

"Please! Don't do anything stupid," pleaded Zif Banjos.

"Stupid? Me?" giggled the man in the lab coat as he zipped up his satchel. "I'm not the one flying to space to eat candy or lording over an island full of monkeys."

"They're lemurs," said Dick Memphis.

"Okay, well, you are all terrible people and you deserve everything that's about to happen to you," said the man in the lab coat as he pressed the red button and activated the explosive device attached to the hatch with a small bang and some sparks. "Thanks, guys. This has been a blast."

The hatch of the space capsule blew off its hinges and wheeled into empty nothingness. The man in the lab coat pressed the button on his pen a second time, and a small rocket activated from the bottom of the device and propelled him out the hatch. He kicked off into space and sent the capsule spinning. The billionaire "astronauts" inside desperately clutched at their throats and frantically gasped for oxygen as the capsule began its descent.

The man in the lab coat adjusted the satchels looped over his shoulder, stretched out his arms and bore witness to the majesty of Earth from above as the sun broke the horizon.

"Someday, all of this will be mine," the man in the lab coat whispered to himself.

How unfair it is, he thought, that a handful of business executives can exploit tax loopholes and wage slaves to hoard enough cold hard cash to fund senseless luxuries like balloon expeditions, monorails, and private space programs while all the average people below labored, struggled, and starved. He chuckled to himself knowing that in nine minutes the world was about to become three billionaires lighter and a much better place.

The man in the lab coat began to fall back to earth. A rush of air whipped at his arms as he plummeted faster and faster towards the ground. He clutched tightly to the satchels as he reached speeds over 500 mph. Somewhere after reaching 670 mph, the man in the lab coat was traveling faster than the speed of sound and produced a sonic boom that was heard for miles. He had reached speeds of 833 mph before his staged parachutes deployed from his backpack. His descent slowed and he gently glided back to Earth.

The man in the lab coat's assistant, a young tattooed woman in tight black leather, a lab coat, and pointed stilettos, sped along a barren highway in a black Escalade. She chased after his GPS signal until visual contact had been made. The man in the lab coat dangled from the primary parachute, a brightly colored rainbow canopy with a big frowny face symbol painted across it. He soared towards the awaiting Escalade, where he skimmed the ground at 60 mph and came to an abrupt stop on his rump.

He detached the parachute, walked to the car, and tossed the satchels in the back seat.

"How was your flight?" asked his assistant in a thick Russian accent.

"First class," chuckled the man in the lab coat as he removed his helmet and disguise. "Now drive."

The Escalade pulled off and drove away down the

empty country road. Moments later, the space capsule smashed into the ground in a nearby field. All that remained of the billionaires in the crater were three red splatters, a broken record, and a few ping pong balls.

⊗ CHAPTER 1

1

Shirtless guys in tight trunks and sexy girls in skimpy bikinis frolicked on the banks of a lazy river on the first day of summer. The sun was hot. Hot boys rubbed sunblock on other hot boys. Several hot girls sunbathed topless on the beach when an obnoxious teenager stole their bikini tops and ran off up the beach. The girls chased after him, topless. And hot.

Mayor Stu Paddick stood before the assembled T.V. and newspaper cameras in a top hat and his mayor sash. Paddick was flanked by his two sexy aides, Ginger and Candy, wearing American flag bikinis, flag sunglasses, and political power ties. A small crowd had gathered and politely applauded.

"As the newly elected mayor, I, Stu Paddick, am proud to declare the Riverside Beach open for the first official day of summer vacation!" cheered the mayor. "As you can see, it's a beautiful day, the beaches are open and everybody is having a wonderful time. Clearly there are no more sharks."

The mayor's step-daughter, Molly Bellmead, an 18-year-old girl from the bad side of town, joined her new crew of classy, rich friends sunbathing. The squad of girls all wore tiny bikinis and took turns applying tanning lotion for the amusement of the cute boys with boners who ogled them from towels nearby.

"When is your step-dad going to leave the river?" asked Muffy Von Fingerbang, the dark-haired de facto leader of the squad, looking at Mayor Paddick over her dark sunglasses.

"He's almost done with his speech," said Molly.

Autumn Puttana snuck a drink from a flask. Autumn was the member of the squad who had done every boy at school worth doing and then moved on to the teachers. She purposefully let one of her nipples slip from her bikini top for the gawking boys as she handed the flask to Muffy. The rest of the squad, Lucy, Mary Jane, Addy, and Poppers took turns posing seductively for the horny little beach boys.

"It's hard to smoke weed and drink beer with parents around, Molly," said Muffy. "As the newest member of the group, you should go get us some more beers."

"Yeah, go get us some beer, Molly," said Autumn.

Molly got up with her purse and headed over to Jimmy the Beer Guy, who was selling ice cold beer from a cooler nearby. A biker gang, the Pen15s, rumbled into the area on motorcycles and interrupted the mayor's speech with a thunderous roar.

Holtie Thump, the bad boy from the good side of town, ran up to talk with Pen15 Club President Harley Auspuffrohr while the Pen15 Gang raised hell up and down the river. Harley, a wiry weasel of a biker with long greasy hair and a thin wet mustache, was the leader of the gang and had been Holtie's late uncle's best friend. Holtie looked up to Harley with the same reverie he had for his uncle and did anything he could to impress Harley and join the Pen15s.

"Hey, Holtie! Why don't you go get us some beers?" said Harley.

"Sure thing, Harley!" Holtie said, cheerfully.

Molly stood by Jimmy the Beer Guy's cooler and pulled out her wallet from her purse.

"What can I get you?" said Jimmy the Beer Guy.

"How much for a six-pack?" asked Molly.

"$40 bucks," said Jimmy, matter of factly.

"$40 dollars!" Molly exclaimed, shocked.

"Hey, a guy's got to eat," said Jimmy.

Mayor Paddick stormed across the beach in the direction that the wild bikers were making a racket.

"Hey, what's the big deal? I'm trying to make a big mayoral speech over here! This is a summer town! Gotta get those summer dollars," Mayor Paddick said and stopped briefly to admire the bikini babes. "Oh, hello, ladies. How would you like to be an intern at City Hall? Ever been with a mayor before?"

Holtie bumped into Molly as she was turning away from Jimmy the Beer Guy. Her lips quivered and tears welled up in her eyes.

"Hey, watch where you're going," said Holtie, acting tough.

Molly started to cry.

"Whoa. Hey. What's wrong?" asked Holtie, a little nicer. "Please, don't cry."

"I don't have enough money for beer," Molly sobbed, "and my new friends, they just started hanging out with me because my step-dad is mayor, and I don't want to disappoint them."

"It's okay, I've got you," said Holtie, pulling out his wallet. "What's your name?"

"Molly Bellmead," she said.

"I'm Holtie," he said. "Holtie Thump. Hey, Jimmy? How much for everything?"

"Cooler and ice, too?" said Jimmy. "$300."

Holtie pulled three crisp $100 bills and a $20 bill out of his wallet and handed them to Jimmy the Beer Guy.

"Here. And a little extra for you," Holtie said to Jimmy. "Now scram!"

"Whatever you say, Holtie," said Jimmy, stuffing the money in his pocket and heading off the beach to get more beer.

Holtie pulled an ice cold six-pack from the cooler and handed it to Molly.

"Thank you," said Molly. "Holtie, was it?"

"Yeah, Holtie. No problem, Molly. I'll see you around," he said.

Holtie picked up the beer cooler with his bulging biceps. He smiled at Molly and headed back towards the biker gang with the cooler. Molly felt butterflies in her stomach and smiled as she carried the six-pack of beer back to her friends.

The mayor's aides flirted and handed out "I'm the MAYOR, bitch!" campaign buttons to several hunky guys in swim trucks flexing to impress the mayor's aides with their muscles. Mayor Paddick didn't even notice, as he flirted with a group of younger girls in bikinis who stood next to a "Danger: River Sharks" sign. It had been months without a river shark attack, but the mayor knew that fragile peace couldn't last forever. Paddick pulled out his cellphone.

"Selfie, ladies?" crowed the mayor, clutching the bikini girls in close for a selfie. "Gotta do it for the gram, am I right?"

"Who the fuck are you?" asked a bikini babe.

"I'm the MAYOR, bitch!" Mayor Paddick yelled, holding out a campaign button with his face on it. "Button?"

Molly found her towel and sat down with the beer next to the squad.

"Hey, give me one of those," said Autumn, rolling over and giving the boys another titillating display.

Molly took a beer and handed the remaining five beers to Autumn, who closed her flask and shoved it under her towel.

"I see you met Holtie," purred Muffy, eyeing the Pen15 bikers. "He's really something, isn't he."

"He seems nice," said Molly.

"Nice? Maybe you never heard of him at your public school, but at our private school he's kind of a big deal," Autumn said and popped her beer open. "I heard one time he got suspended for getting drunk in shop class and trying to fist fight a teacher."

"I heard from one of the guys on the swim team that he's got a nine inch cock," Muffy said and reached for a beer. "He's so dreamy."

Mayor Stu Paddick charged by, aides in tow, and slowed down to check out Molly and her friends in their bikinis.

"Now, those are some fine constituent asses," said the mayor.

"God, Stu!" Molly yelled at her step-dad. "You are so gross."

"Are you going to introduce me to your friends, Molly?" said Stu. "Say, aren't you Jerry Von Fingerbang's daughter?"

"Hi, Mayor Paddick. I'm Muffy. And this is Lucy, Mary Jane, Addy, and Poppers."

"I'm Poppers!" a bubbly Poppers announced.

"I'm Autumn Puttana," said Autumn seductively, as she stood up and got real close to the mayor. "It's a pleasure meeting you, Mr. Mayor."

"Enchanté," said Mayor Paddick, kissing Autumn's hand as he stared down at her cleavage. "Here, have one of my campaign buttons. Why don't I just help you pin that on there…"

The mayor reached to pin an "I'm the MAYOR, bitch!" campaign button on Autumn's bikini top. She stuck her chest out further and fawned as his fingers covertly brushed a nipple.

"Stu!" shouted Molly. "Stop hitting on my friends."

"I see that beer in your hand, Molly" said Paddick.

"I can smell the beer on your breath from here, Stu," retorted Molly.

"Have you paid your taxes?" Stu asked Molly. "I believe you haven't paid your taxes yet."

Molly gave him a stink eye and reluctantly handed her beer over to her step-dad.

"That's right, you're the mayor," Stu said to himself, tapping the beer. "You're the mayor…"

Stu kept walking down the beach to the loud bikers, chugging his beer and groping his scantily clad aides relentlessly as he walked.

"I guess if we're ever going to get drunk we'll just

have to go to the club tonight," said Muffy, watching the mayor go.

Holtie took two beers and set the cooler down in the middle of the Pen15 Gang. The bikers gave Holtie high-fives and patted him on the back. Holtie handed a beer to Harley.

"Look at that! Holtie, my man!" Harley said and clapped Holtie on the shoulder. "How much do we owe ya for the beer?"

"Hey, I just told that beer guy to take a hike and then stole them," Holtie lied as he reverted to being the tough guy.

"Holtie, you're alright," Harley said and took a swig of beer. "And I think you're almost ready to join the gang, man."

Holtie had waited for this day to come for a long time. His uncle had been in the Pen15. This was a family legacy that would have made him proud.

"Really, Harley?" Holtie said, as he barely contained his excitement. "That'd be awesome."

"Yeah, but first we've still got to get you initiated. Get your Pen15 Gang tattoo," said Harley.

Harley held up his right fist to show a weathered Pen15 tattoo on the back of his hand. Two other bikers, Nacho and Jake, both flexed and showed off their Pen15 tattoos to Holtie.

"Penis," snickered a nearby beachgoer at the gang's name.

"Why do people keep doing that?" asked Harley as he looked around confused.

Nacho and Jake, Harley's right and left hand men, slapped Holtie on the shoulders.

"Hey, thanks for the beer, man!" said Nacho.

"What is the meaning of this?" Mayor Paddick said as he stomped up to the biker gang. "Who dares to interrupt my speech? Do you know who I am? I demand to speak to the person in charge here."

"Hey, Nacho? Jake? Who the hell is this guy getting all up in my face?" asked Harley with a sneer.

"I'm the MAYOR, bitc…" said Stu.

"Hey, cool it, Mr. Mayor," Harley interrupted coolly. "We were just getting ready to leave anyway, weren't we?"

"Drink 'em and drop 'em, boys," said Nacho.

The Pen15 Gang hopped on their motorcycles and tossed their empty beer cans at the sputtering mayor as they roared away. Molly and her friends all laughed at Stu as he marched away humiliated with his sexy aides trailing close behind.

2

"Doesn't it seem kind of pointless to be guarding an empty industrial building like this?" Frank asked Joe as he tipped up his faded security guard hat with his flashlight.

The old industrial building had seen better

days. Once it had been home to a semi-successful manufacturer of discount ladies' perfumes, soaps, and shampoos. Now, long abandoned, the building sat empty and the grounds unmaintained.

Joe lit up a joint from his pocket and puffed away at the citrusy sweet smoke, then passed the joint to Frank. The official security company policy was mandatory drug testing, but as the founder, owner, and chief security officer of the "security company", Joe was largely immune from scrutiny. Frank, by way of being Joe's nephew and only employee, was also largely immune from this company policy as well.

"It's a little slower paced than most jobs, yeah," replied Joe.

Frank took a deep drag of the joint and held it. Joe wondered how the kid could do it. The weed he had smoked as a kid wasn't this genetically engineered hydroponic shit. Joe's head was completely swimming after only a couple puffs. But Frank, he could smoke weed endlessly.

"I mean, at least we can get high and fuck off all day on this one," said Frank, between hits.

"It's an easy paycheck, man," said Joe. "Enjoy it."

Frank passed the joint back to Joe, who took a small hit and immediately handed it back to Frank. Joe was sufficiently baked and figured Frank was well on his way.

"I mean, who'd even want to break into a place like this anyway?" said Frank, through a cloud of smoke.

Who indeed.

The dark Escalade pulled up just on the edge of the property, well out of sight of the security guards, and the driver put the vehicle into park. A man in a lab coat stepped out of the passenger side to survey the old industrial building. The driver, his assistant, stepped out of the vehicle wearing high heels and a matching lab coat.

"This is place, yes?" she said, in a thick Russian accent. The assistant reached into the back of the Escalade and pulled out a shovel from beneath a pile of satchels.

"Yes," said the man in the lab coat with a wide toothy grin. "I think this might just be the one."

Nearby, the two security guards finished their joint.

"That was some good weed," said Frank. "I'm already pretty faded."

No shit, thought Joe, barely keeping it together himself.

"Okay, Frank. We better at least make the rounds," said Joe as he dropped the joint to the ground and stepped on it. "I'll go check the loading dock out back. You go around the front and check the doors."

Joe tossed Frank his keys and the two security guards headed in separate directions around the building. As Frank disappeared toward the front doors, Joe held his hand to his mouth, the smell of Marijuana unmistakably on his breath. The security guard pulled a stick of mint gum from his pocket and paused to admire the reflective foil wrapper as it glinted in the midday sun. He popped the gum into his mouth, crumpled up the wrapper and tossed it on the ground.

This is a pretty sweet gig, Joe thought as he ambled toward the loading dock. He turned the corner and his weed numbed brain didn't even have time to process the shovel being swung toward his head by the petite woman in the lab coat. The shovel met Joe's crown with a mighty clonk and left the security guard unconscious and sprawled out on the ground. The woman in the lab coat grabbed the security guard by the ankles and dragged his limp body into the shadows.

Frank was certain he had heard something go clonk on the other side of the building. He peered around the corner in the direction Joe had gone on patrol and didn't see anything.

"It was nothing," said Frank to himself, with a chuckle. "This weed must be making me super paranoid."

Frank turned back around the corner to his appointed rounds and was as prepared for a shovel to the head as his uncle Joe had been. The young security guard was knocked senseless and fell to the ground with a thud. The man in the lab coat reached down with his thick rubber gloved hand and took the keys to the building from Frank. After several attempts in locating the correct key, the man in the lab coat opened the front door of the old industrial building and peered inside.

"Yes, this will do," said the man in the lab coat, silhouetted in the doorway. "This will do quite nicely."

The man in the lab coat ran his thick rubber gloves along a railing and examined the residue as he rubbed it between his fingers. The woman in the lab coat and heels still held the shovel as she stepped in behind him.

"Check the guards for phones and tie them up in the basement," said the man in the lab coat. "I need to tidy a few things up around here before we can begin."

3

Irma Paddick sat on the couch and watched television in a drunken stupor as a cigarette dangled from her pork chop lips. From the curlers in her hair, one might have concluded that she was getting ready to go out somewhere or perhaps was even expecting company. This assumption would be wrong, as indicated by the stained floral housecoat and filthy fuzzy slippers she wore on her calloused feet.

"I had a lot of fun at the river today," said Molly from the kitchen as she poured a cheap bourbon into a glass tumbler full of ice for her mother. "My new friends are nice. Here's your drink, Momma."

"Umbrella," croaked Irma.

As Molly went back into the kitchen in search of a tiny paper cocktail umbrella for her mother's drink, a concerning thought gnawed at the back of her mind. Why would a bunch of spoiled rich kids want to hang out with a poor girl from the wrong side of town anyway?

"I was worried they were only wanting to be my friend because Stu is the Mayor," Molly said. "But they seem cool."

Molly returned to the living room with the paper umbrella and plopped it in Irma's drink between sips.

"Fruit," spat Irma wetly.

"And I met a boy, Momma. He had a motorcycle and the other girls were so jealous he was talking to me."

"Hmmm," grunted Irma. "Motorcycle boys are trouble."

"I know, Momma," said Molly.

"Such a good girl," Irma said and patted Molly's cheek lovingly with her doughy palm.

Mayor Stu Paddick walked through the door. He still wore his mayor's sash and top hat. His aides, Ginger and Candy, followed him in and looked bored as they stood by the door, chilly in their bikinis and power ties.

"Honey I'm home," Stu bellowed and made smoochy faces as he approached Irma. "How about a kiss for your mayor?"

Irma took a big drag on her cigarette and exhaled a cloud of blue smoke directly in Stu's face.

"Hmmm," Irma grunted.

"Yeah, mayoring is a tough job, but somebody's got

to do it. This town would fall to pieces without me holding it together," said Stu. "I'm the... the, um... what's that sticky white stuff that got all over my desk that one time?"

"Cum?!" suggested mayor's aide Ginger.

"Glue, you idiot," corrected mayor's aide Candy.

"That's right! I'm the GLUE that holds this community together!" said Stu, with a certain air of self importance. Molly looked disgusted at Stu as she made her way across the room.

"I'm going to take a shower," Molly said as she headed upstairs. "I'm going out with the girls to the club tonight."

"Hmmm," acknowledged Irma.

Stu took off his top hat and mayor's sash and tossed them toward a hook on the wall. They hit the wall, missed the hook entirely and fell in a heap on the floor.

"So, baby," said Stu. "What's for lunch?"

Irma pulled a fruit skewer from her drink and held it out in front of Stu.

"Fruit," said Irma as she snatched a big hunk of pineapple between her lips and slurped it down her gullet.

"Liquid lunch, it is." said Stu. "You enjoy your fruit. I'm just going to go upstairs and get changed, and I'll pick a little something up for myself later."

The mayor went upstairs. His bikini clad aides

stood awkwardly by the door. Irma sat on the couch, watched T.V. and ignored them coldly.

"So what are you getting paid for this gig?" Candy asked Ginger as she pulled out a nail file and examined her cuticles.

"Paid? Oh, I'm doing it for college credit," said Ginger with a chuckle. She turned to Irma. "Irma, that housecoat really brings out the color of your eyes."

Irma Paddick's eyes slowly swiveled toward Ginger, with her bikini, her perfect body, and smoldering red hair.

"Hmmm," Irma snorted, exhaled a thick cloud of smoke and rolled her watery eyes back toward the television.

***

Molly peeled her shirt off and stood in front of the bathroom mirror in her bikini top as she admired the start of a summer tan on her shoulders. She slipped out of her shorts and turned on the hot water in the shower. Molly took off her bikini top and judged herself harshly in the mirror until her reflection was fogged away by the steam.

The bathroom door was open only a crack, but just enough for Stu to see every inch of his step-daughter's pert young body as he made his way down the hallway to his bedroom. He did a double take and stopped to watch as Molly bent over slowly and wriggled out of her bikini bottom, revealing fresh tan lines on her ass.

Molly put up her hair in an elastic tie to avoid getting her hair wet and slinked toward the shower. She tested the water with her toe and ran her fingers over the stubble of pubic hair along her bikini line. She turned back toward the cabinet beneath the sink to retrieve her razor when she noticed Stu peeking through the slit in the door.

"Stu! I'm your step-daughter, you fucking pervert!" yelled Molly. She grabbed a towel hung from a hook behind the door and clutched it in front of her breasts. Stu straightened up and stepped back from the door.

"Nothing I haven't already seen of yours before. On the internet," chuckled Stu.

"Were you on my page?" Molly said, in total disbelief.

"That's no way to treat a premium subscriber," laughed Stu.

"God, you're gross, Stu!" shrieked Molly as she slammed the bathroom door in his face. Stu shook his head and continued down the hallway to his and Irma's room.

"The mayor's business is the mayor's business," said Stu as he placed a duffel bag on the end of his bed. He looked around the room and picked up one of Irma's dresses and a pair of her high heel shoes from the floor. He stuffed them into the duffel bag and swiftly zipped it closed.

"Mmm hmmm, mayor's business," Stu said, as he headed quickly through the hallway and down the stairs with the duffel bag. Molly, damp and wrapped in a towel, chased down the stairs after him, a flower vase clutched in her hand.

"I'm heading out," Stu shouted to Irma and bolted for the door. "Mayor's business."

"Momma, control your husband!" yelled Molly.

Irma Paddick snored on the couch, a half empty bottle of bourbon clutched in her sausage fingers. Mayor Paddick shooed Candy and Ginger out the door.

"Go, go, go," said Stu.

Molly reached the bottom of the stairs. She held her towel around her naked body with one hand as she threw the flower vase overhanded with the other. Stu slammed the door closed just in time to make his escape. The vase exploded against the door frame and showered the entryway in broken glass and artificial plastic flowers. Irma Paddick woke with a start.

"What? Hmmm," said Irma in a drunken daze.

4

The Pen15 Gang drank, smoked, and partied in the scorching heat of the summer sun at their junkyard biker hangout on the edge of town. Harley Auspuffrohr sat in the shade with his sidekick, Nacho, and downed the last of a lukewarm beer. Nacho nursed a big bottle of vodka. Harley belched loudly and motioned for Holtie Thump to come over and talk with him.

"So, Holtie. If you're real serious about joining the Pen15, I want to be absolutely clear with you about what it is we do. Sit down," said Harley and indicated Holtie should take the  seat next to him. Harley reached over and grabbed a sexy leather clad biker girl with a beer by the waistband. He pulled her roughly into his lap. "Come here, sugar. See Holtie, we drink. We get high. We shoot up. We fuck. We steal."

Harley grabbed the beer from the girl, downed it, and threw the bottle into a fire burning in a nearby steel drum. Harley squeezed the biker girl's large breasts and she bit her lip and giggled playfully at his rough touch.

"We sell drugs. We rape and rob and raise hell. Go get me another beer, baby." said Harley as he pushed the biker girl out of his lap. He slapped her firmly on the ass and she scampered away. Harley turned back to face Holtie. "You are welcome to leave now, Holtie; but once you go through the initiation and get your tattoo, then you're in the Pen15 Gang for life. For life! Do I make myself clear?

"I'm ready, Harley," said Holtie, nervously.

"Okay," said Harley. "Let's do this."

Harley stood up, grabbed the big bottle of vodka from Nacho and handed it to Holtie.

"You're going to need this," said Harley.

A group of bikers formed around Holtie as he sat

down in the chair next to a heavily tattoo-covered biker who held a rusty, old coil tattoo machine. Nacho and Jake grabbed Holtie's shoulders and held him steady, while Holtie took a big swig from the vodka bottle. Holtie started to lower the bottle from his lips, but Harley tipped it right back, which caused Holtie to down a few more shots worth of alcohol. The heavily tattooed biker stoically stomped the footswitch and the tattoo machine buzzed angrily to life.

"There's no going back now. Isn't that right, boys!" yelled Harley.

The assembled crowd of bikers cheered wildly as the needle sank into the back of Holtie's right hand, inking him permanently as a member of the Pen15 Gang. Holtie's head swam with vodka and his hand stung. He winced proudly and held up the finished tattoo for the rest of the Pen15 Gang members to see. The crowd of bikers cheered.

"Now for the initiation," Harley snarled. His eyes darted wildly around the crowd, before coming to a stop on Holtie. "And as much as it hurts me to do this, it's definitely going to hurt you."

Harley held up a long paddle and slapped it against the palm of his hand menacingly. Once again, Nacho and Jake grabbed Holtie's arms, forcing him to bend over the hood of a broken, old junkyard car. Holtie's hands burned on the hot rusted metal of the old car, and at least temporarily, made him forget all about the pain of the freshly inked Pen15 tattoo.

"I've been waiting for my turn to do this for a

long time," laughed Harley, swinging the paddle into Holtie's ass full force. The paddle struck Holtie's left buttock with a nauseatingly loud crack.

Holtie looked back terrified at the paddle and then down at his Pen15 tattoo. Harley twirled the paddle around in his hand and then took another swing, which met Holtie's right ass cheek with another bruising blow. Holtie howled in pain. Harley held the paddle in the air and the Pen15 Gang cheered. With lightning speed, Harley unexpectedly swung the paddle once more, squarely hitting both of Holtie's cheeks with a thundering slap.

"Alright! He's in! Holtie Thump is officially in the Pen15 Gang!" yelled Harley. "Now, let's go to the club and let's get fucking wasted."

Holtie tried to straighten up, but his ass was on fire. He leaned against the hot car and burned his elbow. Two biker girls appeared on either side of Holtie and he leaned on their shoulders just to remain upright. Holtie's head sloshed drunkenly as one of the girls kissed him directly on the lips. Holtie smiled big. He was Pen15 for life and life was good.

⊗ CHAPTER 2

1

Joe woke with a start and his head throbbed. He had been in the security business for nearly two full decades and never once had he ever felt in danger. The kinds of places Joe guarded now were easy money. Vacant warehouses, empty mansions, abandoned factories, with the occasional bar mitzvah or quinceañera gig when the pay was good.

The only exception to the rule for Joe was desolate shopping malls. Malls were something he was no longer interested in guarding, no matter how good the pay. These days there were just too many Mall Ninjas. Joe shuddered at the thought.

Joe was not accustomed to encountering people while on the job more threatening than a wino or maybe some teenagers getting freaky behind a dumpster. But this? This was madness.

Still dizzy, he reached for his radio. Gone. He reached for his phone. Also gone. And there was something around his ankle. He looked down and saw some kind of manacle and chain attached to his leg. The chain was threaded through a support beam and connected by a manacle to his nephew Frank's ankle. Joe tried to pry himself free from the shackle, but it was solid metal and of sturdy construction. Frank stirred awake and clutched his head.

"They took our phones," said Joe.

Frank shook his head and tried to focus his eyes. He grabbed at the manacle around his ankle, panicked and tried to pull his foot loose. Frank squinted and saw a dark figure in the hallway.

"I tried that," said Joe.

The dark figure slunk into the room but remained in the shadows. The two security guards could not make out his face, but they saw the glint of light dance across the dark lenses of his black goggles. The man wore a lab coat and thick black rubber gloves.

"Hello. I see someone is finally up from their nap" said the shadowy man in the lab coat. "So terribly sorry for the blunt force trauma to your skulls. My assistant is very powerful for her size."

"Please," begged Frank. "You have to let us go, man."

"Oh, absolutely," the man in the lab coat said and tossed a rusty old hacksaw saw between Frank and Joe.

"What's that for?" asked Frank.

"That's to cut your legs off," said the man in the lab coat as he stifled a chuckle.

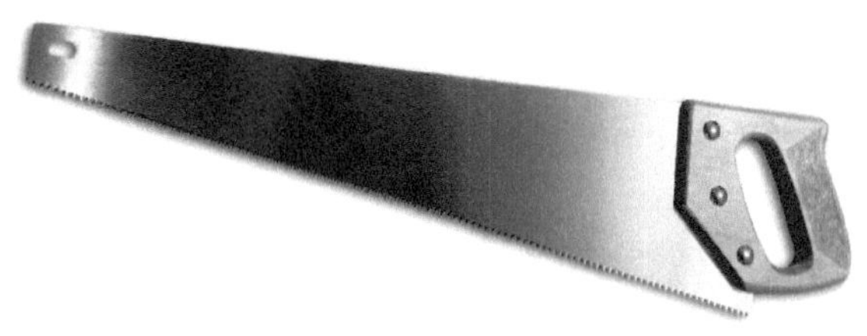

"Like, in *Saw*?" Asked Joe. "So, is this like a *Saw* situation?"

"No, this is nothing like *Saw*," grumbled the man in the lab coat.

"It's just, you chain us up and give us a saw and then tell us to cut our legs off," said Frank. "That's basically the plot of *Saw*."

"It's not like *Saw*," said the man in the lab coat.

"It does kind of remind me of *Saw*," said Frank.

"Enough foolishness," snapped the man in the lab coat. "Now cut your legs off."

The man in the lab coat receded into the shadowy hall and left Joe and Frank alone in the dark basement. They both looked at the saw and then at each other.

"So do you still have any of that weed left?" asked Frank. Joe reached into his security guard hat and pulled out a small bag of joints and a book of matches.

"It's my emergency stash," said Joe.

"This is definitely an emergency," said Frank.

2

The Von Fingerbangs, Jerry & Kitty, lived in a very nice house in a very nice neighborhood. They drove very nice cars, ate very nice food, and belonged to very nice community organizations. They had very nice kids, very nice educations, got very nice jobs, and maintained very nice business relationships. They had very nice teeth, very nice hair, and generally looked very nice, due in large part to their very nice genetics. But they were very shitty people, personality-wise, but how could anyone tell after seeing just how very nice things seemed to be for the Von Fingerbangs.

Molly sat beside Muffy Von Fingerbang in her very nice bedroom and put on makeup in a very nice vanity mirror. Molly looked hard at herself in the mirror again. She knew she came from poor stock and nothing would ever be "very nice" for her. But as she mimicked Muffy, putting on her makeup in the same way Muffy did; she thought she could see a glimmer of something very nice, if not downright better.

The squad of girls prepared themselves for a night of clubbing. Addy and Lucy, naked except for their tiny thong underwear, rifled through Muffy's closet and looked through her very nice collection of last season's dresses. Autumn opened the window, lit a joint, and put on her bra.

"Here, Autumn," said Muffy. "Give me a hit of that."

Autumn took one more long drag and passed the

joint to Muffy. Mary Jane finished drying her hair and handed the blow dryer to Poppers, who stood soaking wet in a towel after a shower. Autumn breathed a cloud of smoke toward the ceiling.

"I'm so fucking horny," said Muffy. "I just want to get laid tonight."

"Me too," said Lucy. "It's been ages."

"There has to be some hot guys at the club tonight," Autumn said as the last of the smoke dissipated above her.

"If I don't find a dick to ride soon, I'm going to have to get one of you drunk and fuck you instead," laughed Muffy. She raised two fingers to her mouth, miming a vagina, and licked between her fingers in Molly's direction. Molly made a disapproving face.

"Here," Molly said and handed Muffy a hairbrush. "Just use this."

The girls all laughed. Poppers finished drying her hair, removed her towel and bounced to the closet naked, where Lucy and Addy modeled dresses for each other. Mary Jane joined Muffy and Molly as they put their makeup on in front of the mirror.

"Molly has Holtie's attention anyway," said Muffy, exhaling as she handed the last of the joint to Mary Jane.

"Now, I'll eat your pussy out after a couple shots," Autumn said to Muffy, with a smile. Muffy caressed on a bright red lipstick, puckered up, and licked her lips.

"That Holtie Thump is exactly the kind of stud I'd like to get my lips around," said Muffy.

3

The prostitutes on main street were a very mixed bag. On any given night you could find pretty, expensive young girls looking for drug money. There were the affordable but tired soccer moms who pimped themselves out for shoe and latte money. There were the haggard old whores that would do anything for almost nothing because they simply knew no other way of life. On the other end of the spectrum were the drag queens, an even further mixed bag of thrill seekers, rent makers, and shoe buyers.

"Hey, daddy," the drag queen called Ms. Carmelita said to a potential John walking down the street. "Looking for a date tonight?"

The man checked her out, shook his head politely and kept moving. He was more interested in girls that could pass for real women. Most of the straight and bisexual guys that the drag queens frequently encountered on the street were looking for someone that their straight brains could justify as being fully female, while still looking to scratch an itch only a dick could reach.

"Hey, honey," the drag queen called Lady Midnight said to the John. "Let's have some fun."

"Hey, baby," said the John, eyeballing Lady

Midnight from head to toe and back again. She was all woman and then some.

"I'll suck your cock for $20 bucks," said Mayor Stu Paddick to the John. Stu wore makeup, a pearl necklace, and sparkly earrings. Stu hiked up the dress he had taken from Irma to show the John some leg and the high heel shoes he had also taken from Irma.

"Uh," said the John, flabbergasted. "No thanks, man."

"Okay," said Stu. "$15 dollars."

The John looked at Stu in his dress, shook his head and started to walk away down the sidewalk.

"Sorry," said the John. "No."

"$10 dollars and I'll jiggle your balls," exclaimed Stu. "Pinky up the pooper. Whatever you're into. Alabama steamroller. Hide the Twinkie. Trap the clam. You name it."

Stu reached into his purse, also borrowed from Irma, and handed the John a business card. The plain card only had "City Hall" printed on it.

"Call me?" said Stu. The John dropped the card and walked quickly away from the drag queen prostitutes. Stu picked up the business card and put it back in his purse. Ms. Carmelita and Lady Midnight exchanged annoyed glances.

"Now, why'd you have to go and scare my trick away?" said Lady Midnight.

"Take your ugly ass somewhere else and stop grossing out the clientele," Ms. Carmelita yelled at Stu.

"Listen, I'm the Mayo… I mean, I have every right to be here," said Stu, defensively. "It's a public sidewalk."

"Bitch, look at you," snapped Lady Midnight. "You haven't even shaved off your damn beard."

"Buh-bye," said Ms. Carmelita.

"This is an outrage," cried Stu. "I'm an honest gal out for a night on the town, just trying to make a little money sucking some dicks, and this is the kind of harassment I get?"

Ms. Carmelita and Lady Midnight both stared at Stu with icy cold looks of disgust.

"I'll complain about this," yelled Stu, clutching his pearls. "I'll go all the way to the top. All the way to the Mayor's office!"

"You do that, bitch," said Lady Midnight.

"Buh-Bye," said Ms. Carmelita.

Stu held his head high as he walked a little further down the sidewalk. He stopped and pulled out a tube of lipstick from Irma's purse, thickly reapplied it and dropped it back into the purse with a snap.

From a black Escalade parked nearby, a shadowy man in a lab coat used a camera with a big zoom lens to snap several pictures of Mayor Stu Paddick dressed in drag in his wife's clothing. The man in the lab coat creaked with laughter.

"I think we probably have enough," said the man. "Drive."

The man in the lab coat's assistant popped the Escalade into gear and drove away down Main Street slowly.

4

Harley, Holtie, and the Pen15 gang sat in a big booth at the club, where they covertly vaped and drank beer by the bucket.

"No hard feelings about the paddling," said Harley to Holtie. "I mean, I even had to do it myself once."

A young club waitress with colorfully dyed hair named Brandy bent over to clear a table. Harley eyed her butt hungrily. Brandy picked up her tip money from the table and slipped it into her bra. Harley got up from his booth and stood directly behind her. As Brandy reached across the table for an empty glass, Harley lifted her skirt up and exposed her tight ass and a lacy pair of purple panties. Brandy whirled around to slap Harley and he caught her by the wrist.

"Hey, watch it buddy," yelled Brandy, a tired look on her face that said this kind of thing happened all too often.

"Hey, baby," said Harley, coolly. "Why don't you go get us another round of beers."

Harley spun Brandy around and slapped her ass as she walked quickly away from the table to the bar where Sam, the bartender, was training in a new server named Poindexter.

"Hey, Sam. Those biker dudes just ordered another bucket of beer," said Brandy. "But they've been harassing me. The little loud one just grabbed my ass. What do you want me to do with them?"

"Sorry, Brandy," Sam the bartender said, apologetically. "Poindexter, go take over that table from Brandy."

"Right away, Sam," Poindexter said, with a kind of nasally optimism and can-do spirit mustered only by someone on their first "real" job. Poindexter filled a bucket with ice and beer.

Molly and the rest of the squad had placed their orders and waited by the bar. Brandy swiftly passed each girl her drink over the counter.

"Here you go, guys," said Brandy, sliding a vodka diet across the bar to Molly and something fruity and colorful to Poppers.

"Thanks," said Molly.

"I'm Poppers," said Poppers.

"You sure are," said Brandy.

The other girls went to find a place to sit and scope out boys while Molly dug around in her purse for a tip for Brandy. Molly only came back with change, which she apologetically left on the bar and went to join her friends on the other side of the club. Muffy waved Molly over and Addy pointed across the room to where Holtie and the Pen15s were gathered.

"Over there," said Addy with a smile. "Looks like your boyfriend is here, Molly."

"God, I want to ride his cock so bad," growled Muffy. She turned to Molly. "Hey, come outside and smoke with me."

Muffy grabbed Molly by the arm and dragged her

outside, just as Poindexter brought the bucket of beer to the rowdy biker's table.

"Here's your beer, sir," said Poindexter.

"Hey, where's that hot waitress?" asked Harley. "The chick waiting on us before?"

Holtie, Nacho, and Jake emptied the bucket of beer bottles. Poindexter squirmed, too new on the job to know what to do next, he hoped this would be the end of this interaction. Harley stared at him like a tiger ready to lunge at a plump gazelle.

"Your waitress said you made her feel uncomfortable," said Poindexter. Harley stood up out of the booth, picked up the empty ice bucket and got right in Poindexter's face.

"Oh, is that so?" said Harley. "Well, I wouldn't want to make anyone feel uncomfortable."

"Listen, fellas, I don't want any trouble," stammered Poindexter.

"There won't be any trouble," said Harley, as he cornered the flinching Poindexter. "Just so long as the hot waitress gets her pretty little ass back over here with another bucket of beer."

Harley raised the ice bucket and dumped it over Poindexter's head. Ice cubes and freezing cold water ran down the young server's tucked-in shirt and pooled in his butt crack. Poindexter shivered, sputtered, and spit out a mouthful of water. Sam the bartender pulled a baseball bat from behind the counter, banged it behind the counter and held it aloft for the whole Pen15 gang to see.

"That's it," bellowed Sam. "You guys can get the fuck out of my bar!"

"That's cool," said Harley. "We were just leaving anyway. Isn't that right, Nacho?"

"Yeah, fuck this place," said Nacho in agreement.

The bikers got up from their booth and followed Harley as he went outside. Jake downed his beer and threw the bottle in the direction of Sam the bartender. The bottle exploded into tiny wet fragments against a stool beside the bar.

"Real cool, guys," said Sam.

Before going out the door, Nacho turned and swiped everything off a customer's table, spilling drinks and appetizers onto the floor. Holtie picked up a napkin from another table, tore it into tiny pieces and tossed it in the air like confetti in the entryway.

Outside the club, the Pen15 Gang made their way to their bikes. As Holtie exited the club, he saw Molly vaping weed and Muffy smoking a cigarette on the sidewalk. Molly turned, spied Holtie and smiled.

"Hey, Holtie," Molly said as she exhaled a plume of vapor.

"Oh, hey," said Holtie. "Molly, right?"

"Hey, Holtie," flirted Muffy as she undressed Holtie with her eyes and savored the bulge in his pants.

"Are you just leaving?" asked Molly.

"We've got biker gang stuff to do," explained Holtie. "Mind if I have a hit of that?"

Molly handed the vape to Holtie. Holtie took a quick puff and licked his lips as he exhaled. The vape tasted like lavender, but there was something else. He took another longer drag and passed it back to Molly.

"It tastes like your chapstick," said Holtie.

"Sorry," said Molly.

"No, I like it," said Holtie. "Hey, what are you doing tomorrow night?"

"We're not doing anything," said Muffy as she batted her eyelashes sexily at Holtie. Holtie barely noticed Muffy and stared at Molly as she inhaled a big chestful of sweet calming weed vapor into her lungs and exhaled slowly.

"We're having a party tomorrow night at the Pen15 hangout," said Holtie. "Maybe you and your friends want to come?"

Muffy ran her hand over Holtie's muscular chest and breathed in deeply the musky smell of his sweat.

"I want to come, Holtie," Muffy said, coyly.

"I'd like to see you again," said Molly.

Holtie took a pen out of his jacket pocket. He looked around for something to write on and tore off a piece of a flyer hanging on a light pole. Holtie wrote down the address and his phone number and handed the scrap of paper to Molly.

"Here," said Holtie, nervously smiling at Molly. "See you tomorrow?"

Molly smiled back at Holtie and bit her lip. The Pen15 Gang was ready to ride and fired up their motorcycles. Harley waved for Holtie to follow.

"Come on!" Harley said. "Let's get out of here!"

"I've got to go," said Holtie.

"See you tomorrow," Molly said as she clutched the paper tightly in her hand.

Holtie hopped on his motorcycle and roared away from the nightclub with Harley and the Pen15 Gang.

"Oh my god," Muffy said as she smoked her cigarette. "I want him inside me."

Molly ignored her and took another hit of weed.

5

The shadowy man in the lab coat added vials and jars of strange chemicals to a large steaming mixing vat. The thick yellowish green ooze bubbled and foamed as the man used a giant metal spoon to stir the goo with his big rubber gloved fists.

The man's eyebrows furrowed and he motioned for his assistant to bring him a beaker of glowing green chemicals, labelled with XXX, a skull and crossbones, and a frowny face. Taking the beaker in his free hand, the man in the lab coat peered inside at what he most certainly knew to be a sloshing horror mere inches from his face. He tilted the beaker and poured the luminous liquid into the green slime that festered in the mixing vat. The fluid in the vat glowed intensely as the chemicals swirled together.

"I did it, Missy!" yelled the man in the lab coat with a cackle of delight at his success. "I did it! The formula is complete!"

His assistant, Missy Gore, rolled her eyes and stepped back as the man in the lab coat spun into a wild frenzied celebratory dance. He excitedly grabbed a pipette resting next to a flower pot from the countertop, dipped it into the sludge, and extracted a small amount of the glowing green liquid. The man in the lab coat walked back over to the potted plant on the counter and added a single drop of green ooze to the soil in the pot.

Missy Gore stood beneath a "No Smoking" sign, lit a cigarette, and watched with disinterest as the dirt in the pot began to bubble and froth. Green vapors rose from the potted plant, and then the flower itself burst into flames.

"Most interesting," said the man in the lab coat. "Yes, most interesting indeed."

The man began to laugh maniacally as the flames licked the plant's leaves, burning brighter and brighter. Missy Gore rolled her eyes again, walked out of the laboratory and left the man in the lab coat alone to savor his latest misguided scientific discovery.

6

Frank and Joe passed a joint back and forth and talked about life's big mysteries as the rusty saw laid between them.

"Trust me, man," posited Frank. "*Saw 4* was way, way better than *Saw 3*."

"Was there even a saw in either of those movies," asked Joe.

"I don't think it needs to have a saw to be a *Saw* movie," said Frank. Missy Gore entered the room smoking her cigarette.

"Hey, it's the shovel lady," Joe said cheerfully, suddenly remembering their predicament. "You should probably let us go."

"Do you have anything to eat?" asked Frank.

"No, Frank. We can go get something to eat when she lets us go," Joe said as he puffed on the joint. "Right, shovel lady? Let us go get you something to eat."

"Crunchwraps, man," said Frank.

Missy Gore dropped her cigarette to the ground

and stomped it out under her severely spiky black stilettos. She reached into a box on a table and pulled out two big cans of canned pasta, which she tossed at the security guard's feet.

"Whoa, mini ravioli. That sounds good, too," said Frank as he held up the cans for his uncle to see. "Look, Joe. Mini beef ravioli. Family size."

"What are we supposed to use to open the cans?" asked Joe. Missy Gore pointed to the saw on the floor.

"Saw!" Missy Gore said indignantly, in a thick Russian accent. Joe and Frank both looked down at the saw and then confusedly at each other.

"Right," Joe said apprehensively.

"Cut your legs off!" yelled Missy Gore. She turned, stormed out of the room, and left the security guards alone in the basement with the saw and the family size cans of mini beef ravioli.

"Well, that was awful nice of her," Frank said as he picked up one of the cans and tried to cut the can down the middle with the saw. Joe realized his nephew was otherwise occupied and looked around the basement.

"Where are we supposed to pee?" asked Joe.

7

Karen Thump sat at her kitchen counter in front of a large bowl of fresh green salad and stared at the clock. She took an assortment of pills prescribed to her by her doctor and washed them down with a tumbler of vodka. Karen heard her son's motorcycle rumble up the street, followed by the sound of keys at the door. Holtie assumed his mother was already asleep, tip-toed into the house, and set his jacket and keys on a chair.

"Where have you been?" asked Karen as she slowly swirled her tumbler of ice and booze.

"Hey, Mom," said Holtie. "You're up awfully late."

"God damn it, Holton," Karen spat. "Where have you been?"

"I was just out with some friends," explained Holtie.

"Is that what you plan to do with your life, Holton? Hang out with your friends?"

"No, Mom. I was just…"

"You need to get your life together, Holton," Karen scolded. "Get a job. Start applying to business schools."

As Holtie shifted back and forth, Karen noticed the Pen15 tattoo on the back of his right hand. Her mouth dropped open.

"What is that?" Karen gasped.

"Nothing, Mom," Holtie said and then quickly tried to hide his hand. The cat was already out of the bag. Karen seized his wrist.

"You are grounded," said Karen. Her face grew red and the veins began to stand out on her forehead and neck.

"You can't ground me," said Holtie. "I'm over 18."

"Ever since your father killed himself, this has been my house," yelled Karen. "My house, my rules."

"That is so unfair. I was just making new friends…"

"Unfair?" Karen said, perplexed. "As long as you are under my roof you will obey me."

"That is so fucking stupid," mumbled Holtie.

"Excuse me?"

"I said that is so fucking stupid! I don't even want to go to business school. Why can't I just take a little time off before thinking about college. Jesus!"

"I won't let you throw away your future hanging out at the river all day like some…"

"What!" yelled Holtie. "Like a what, Mom?"

"Like a bottom dweller," screamed Karen. "Like river litter. Like some kind of bum!"

Holtie started to yell something, stopped, then grabbed his keys and jacket, and made for the door.

"You know what?" said Holtie as he flung the door open.

"Get back here, young man!" commanded Karen.

"I'm going out!" Holtie said as he slammed the door behind him.

"You come back here this instant!" shrieked Karen.

Karen picked up her salad bowl and tossed it against the wall in frustration. Seething, she grabbed the next closest thing, her tumbler of vodka. Karen downed the whole glass and fell into a kitchen chair, where she wept into the countertop.

8

Harley grabbed Kimber's hips and pushed his penis balls-deep into her dripping pink pussy. Kimber's legs shook and she moaned with pleasure. Jake stepped around a junked car and tried to slip in line before Nacho.

"No way, man," Nacho said and used his big tattooed hand to shove Jake back. "Me next."

Holtie roared his bike into the Pen15's junkyard. He still shook from the confrontation with his mother. Holtie was pushed beyond the point of exhaustion. He looked at the Pen15 tattoo on the back of his hand in the light of a bonfire burning in a rusty metal drum. Who needs business school, he thought and sauntered into the biker hangout.

"Hey, man," Holtie said with a nod to Harley. "Do you mind if I crash here tonight?"

"Mi casa is su casa," said Harley, between thrusts. "You're in the Pen15 now. You're always welcome."

Holtie gave a thumbs up and started to make his way through the biker orgy. Harley stopped fucking Kimber for a moment.

"You look a little sad, Holtie," Harley said while his penis throbbed inside the girl's sweet slit. "You want to take a turn riding Kimber?"

"No, I'm good," said Holtie.

"I could just blow you," said Kimber. "It's family style."

"Maybe another night," said Holtie and continued his walk to the back of the junkyard.

"Suit yourself, man," Harley said as he exploded hot cum inside of Kimber with a primal grunt. "Hooooooo!"

Holtie saw an abandoned mattress sticking out from behind a car fender and walked towards it. Holtie took off his jacket and longed for sleep. But as he rounded the car he noticed two large half-naked bikers, one with a handlebar mustache and the other with a scruffy beard, as they made out on the mattress.

"Occupied," said the biker with the handlebar mustache.

"It's okay. You're good guys," said Holtie. "Don't mind me. As you were."

Holtie balled up his jacket, lay down, and rolled over to try to sleep on the end of the mattress.

"Want to join us?" asked the scruffy bearded biker.

"No, man. I'm good," said Holtie.

"If you want, we could just blow you," said the biker with the handlebar mustache. "It's family style."

"Maybe another night," said Holtie, sleepily.

"Suit yourself," said the scruffy bearded biker.

Holtie closed his eyes and tried to sleep, while the bikers kissed and rolled around on the mattress. The biker with the handlebar mustache gagged somewhere in the darkness.

"Oh, suck that cock, yeah baby," moaned the biker with the scruffy beard. The sounds of sucking and choking persisted. Then the mattress began to shake.

"Spit on it first and go slower," said the biker with the handlebar mustache, somewhere in the darkness. "Oh, that's it. Oh! Yeah! Fuck yeah! Fuck me, Daddy!"

Holtie relaxed and drifted off to slumber.

☹ CHAPTER 3

1

Bikers in various states of undress were sprawled out across the junkyard as the sunrise broke the horizon. A loud car horn honked just at the edge of the Pen15 hangout.

The man in the lab coat stepped out of the back of the black Escalade, and his bald head shined in the early morning sunlight. The lab coat hid his powerfully large muscles but could not conceal his flabbily large gut. He stroked his long red beard, streaked with white hairs, and adjusted his impenetrably black goggles.

Missy Gore honked the Escalade's horn again. Nacho awoke first, still hungover, and climbed out of a sea of naked biker girls. He shook Jake awake.

"Did you hear that, man?" asked Nacho.

"Hear what?" said Jake. Missy Gore honked the horn again.

"That, man," said Nacho.

"Will you two shut the fuck up?" groaned Harley

from somewhere within the naked girl sea. Missy Gore honked the horn again. Harley put on a shirt and marched to the gate, Nacho and Jake shuffled after him. Harley stumbled into the bright sunlight and eyed the man in the lab coat warily.

"Hello, biker gang," said the man in the lab coat.

"Who the fuck are you and what the fuck do you want?" asked Harley.

"My name is Doctor Frownyface," said the man in the lab coat. "And I'd like to be friends."

Harley scrunched up his face in confusion. Doctor Frownyface smiled broadly and revealed a row of yellow, stained teeth. He held up his thick rubber gloved hand and dangled a big plastic bag of pill bottles for the Pen15 Gang to see.

2

The girls were all spread out on the floor of the hot yoga studio. Molly laid her yoga mat down next to Muffy's and began to stretch. Karen Thump entered the studio in tights and a spandex leotard. She wore sweatbands on her forehead and wrists in the 105°F heat of the hot yoga studio, and already she dripped with sweat. The girls got on their hands and knees as the yoga instructor swished into the room and walked among them.

"Good puppy dog stretches," said the instructor. "Really get those butts in the air."

"Are you excited for the party tonight?" whispered Lucy.

"Some of those bikers looked sexy as fuck," whispered Autumn as she smiled. "All muscly and covered in tattoos. Real bad boys."

"And someone's pretty much guaranteed to get laid tonight," whispered Muffy to Molly.

"Guys," said Molly.

"Shhhhhhhh!" hissed Karen at the girls, annoyed by the disturbance.

"Let's turn it over and do some bridge poses," the yoga instructor said, as the girls all flipped into position on their backs. "Thrust those pelvises and get your butts off the ground. And arch those backs, ladies."

Shoulders on the floor and feet flat and even with their hands, the girls and Karen began to thrust their pelvises in the air. Autumn felt dizzy and lay flat on her back, hand held to her forehead. Mary Jane looked over and saw Autumn woozily sit up. The yoga instructor ran over to check on her.

"You look like you're going to faint, Autumn," said Mary Jane.

"Are you okay, sweetheart?" asked the yoga instructor. Autumn nodded and held her hand on her forehead in an attempt to steady the room.

"I'm fine," she said. "I think I just got a little dizzy from the heat."

"Why don't you go get some water and cool down

in the shower?" said the yoga instructor. "Mary Jane, can you help her out?"

Autumn grabbed her yoga mat and left the yoga studio with Mary Jane while the other girls looked on with concern.

"Release that tension, girls!" barked the yoga instructor as he momentarily regained their attention. "I want to see you releasing that tension in your backs before your butt cheeks touch the floor!"

"I saw the way he was looking at you last night," whispered Muffy to Molly.

"He seems really nice," whispered Molly.

"But I'd still let him stick it in my ass the first chance I get," purred Muffy.

"Shhhhhhhhhhhhhhhhhh!" Karen scolded the girls angrily.

3

Harley held the pill bottle up to his eyes and examined the tiny green pills inside. He shook the bottle, rattled the pills, and then stared harder with a look of frustration at the frowny face logo on the side of the bottle.

"I don't get it," said Harley, quizzically. "If these pills are as good as this Frownyface guy says they are, then why didn't he want anything for them?"

"Free drugs are free drugs," said Nacho.

"Whatever. Here, Jake," said Harley. "Take one of these and tell me what it's like."

Harley tossed the pill bottle to Jake, who anxiously opened the bottle and took one. Jake tossed the bottle back to Harley and waited for the effects of the pill to kick in.

Holtie woke up on the mattress, sandwiched between the biker with the handlebar mustache and the biker with the scruffy beard. He rubbed his jaw, picked up his jacket and walked toward the front of the junkyard, where Harley and the rest of the Pen15 Gang stood around and watched Jake.

"My man. How's your ass?" asked Harley.

"A little stretched out," replied Holtie.

"What? No, I meant from the paddling initiation," said Harley.

"Oh, right. It's good," said Holtie. "And my hand hurts less. Like a sunburn now."

"Hey, I might have a little job for you. A chance to make some real money," said Harley as he handed a pill bottle to Holtie. "This guy just brought us some drugs."

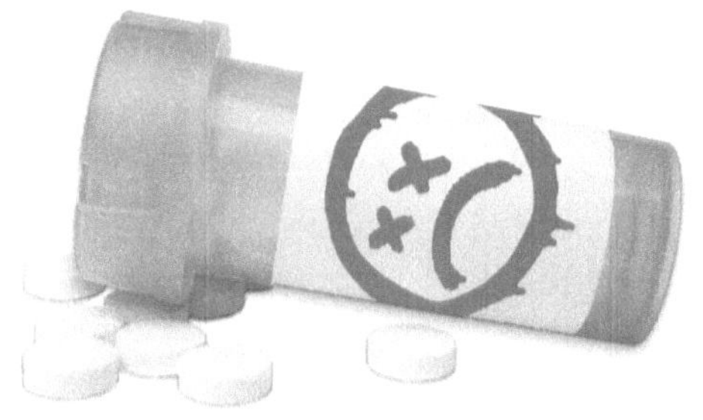

"What are they?" asked Holtie.

"He called them Dopiods. So new they're not illegal, but so scarce that our little club is the only supplier in town." explained Harley. "I want you to take some out, try to sell them to your friends or down at the river, then bring me back the money. Don't worry, you'll get your cut."

"What do they do?" asked Holtie. Harley pointed to Jake, who stood motionless. Completely zoned out, Jake drooled down his chin with a distant look in his eyes.

"They do that," said Harley. "Appears to be some pretty powerful shit."

Harley gave Jake a little shove and laughed as the doped up biker fell over without any resistance, stiff as a board.

4

Muffy rinsed the soap from her body and stepped out of the locker room shower. The air was cooler than the heat of the yoga studio, and her nipples stood at attention from the stark difference in temperature. Molly finished getting dressed at her locker and joined Autumn as she put on her makeup at the mirror. She watched in the mirror reflection as Muffy dried her perfect body with a towel. Molly felt flush with self-awareness.

"Molly, I was wondering if I could ask your advice on something," Autumn said.

"Sure, Autumn," said Molly. "What is it?"

"I missed my period for a few months. So I, well, I took a pregnancy test," Autumn said as she pulled a pregnancy test from her makeup bag and showed it to Molly.

"It's positive, Autumn," Molly said, with a look of shock.

"The first one was positive, so I took another test. It was positive, too," said Autumn. "This is actually the third one I've tried. I think I'm pregnant."

"What are you going to do," asked Molly.

"I don't know," said Autumn. "That's what I was hoping to ask your advice on."

"Do you know who the father is?" asked Molly.

"I think it might be Jimmy, but it might be Brian, but it could be Robert, or maybe Dusty. Mmmm," Autumn said, growing more and more excited by the thought of each sexual encounter.

"Autumn!" Molly said.

Karen Thump wore a thick terry cloth robe and towel on her head as she joined the two girls at the mirror.

"Right," said Autumn. "So I don't know what to do."

"Have you considered an abortion? Because you are an absolute train wreck," said Molly.

"I know," said Autumn.

The mere mention of abortion was like a dog whistle to Karen's ears. She barely contained her outrage as she listened to the girls talk about the subject so casually. Her eyebrows went up in shock.

"Maybe I could get a DNA test done?" said Autumn.

"Why?" asked Molly.

Addy walked over to the mirror topless, examined her boobs, and began to freshen up her makeup.

"Well, a couple of the guys I've fucked recently are pretty rich," said Autumn plainly. "Robert had a huge cock and his dad owns a car dealership."

"His dick isn't that big," Addy said as she brushed on mascara.

Karen's eyes grew huge at this revelation. She turned from the mirror and tried to go back to her locker, but a topless Poppers stood in her way.

"I'm Poppers," said Poppers.

Karen stormed around her in a huff. Addy finished her makeup, teased her hair, and returned to her locker.

"It's your choice, Autumn," said Molly. "But I'd think about it carefully."

The girls got dressed and made their way outside.

"Are you feeling better, Autumn?" asked Lucy.

"Yeah, it was nothing to worry about. I'll get it taken care of soon," said Autumn.

"Let's meet back at my place," said Muffy as she strutted down the sidewalk. "Bring your suits."

5

Nacho and Holtie parked their bikes on the street outside a massage parlor and walked up the sidewalk to a spot outside the hot yoga studio, where Nacho quickly sold another bottle of Dopiods to a young couple, the Smiths. Nacho took their money, handed over a bottle of green pills, and the couple was on their way. Holtie couldn't believe it was just that easy to sell drugs to people on the street. It turned out that just the mention of drugs was enough for most people to get out their wallets. Holtie and Nacho had already managed to move more than half of the pills they had received from Harley.

"Hey, I'm going to go try to sell to some of my old high school friends," said Holtie, giving Nacho a fist bump.

"Cool beans," said Nacho, with a wave.

Holtie took off down the street, a spring in his step. Another young couple walked down the street. Nacho could tell they were squares and his pitch lacked the usual enthusiasm.

"Hey, man. You guys do pills?" whispered Nacho. "I got Dopiods, man."

The square couple ignored him and continued down the street. Karen Thump stepped out of the hot yoga studio, and Nacho had a good feeling just looking at her. He knew from past experience that high-strung, middle-aged career women tended to avoid alcohol because of all the calories and favored pills more for the freaky shit they liked to do when they unwound.

"Hey, lady. You into pills?" whispered Nacho to Karen. "Maybe the e-sex scene? I got them pills."

"What?" gasped Karen.

"Dopiods, man," crooned Nacho. "I got what you need."

"Well, I never!" huffed Karen as she clutched her purse and stormed off up the street.

6

The security guards had fallen asleep on the old industrial building's basement floor. A half dozen smoked joints had been extinguished between their feet. Missy Gore kicked in the door and stormed into the room. Joe was the first to wake up.

"Hey, please. Please, let us go!" begged Joe.

"Shut your mouth," Missy Gore said in her thick Russian accent. Doctor Frownyface glided into the room.

"Hmmm? What?" Frank said, waking up. His mouth was covered in ravioli sauce. He pointed at a wet spot on the floor. "That's the pee area."

"Listen, man. Just let us go and I promise we won't tell anyone," pleaded Joe.

"That's the poop area," said Frank as he pointed at a turd on the floor, just at the end of his leg chain's reach.

"Did you poop on the floor?" asked Missy Gore.

"Well, that's what happens when you give someone a family size can of mini beef ravioli and no bathroom."

"I'm begging you," Joe said as he sparked up a half-smoked joint. "I have fish. I need to get home and feed my fish."

"We have a bathroom, you know?" said Doctor Frownyface as he looked at Frank's feces in disgust.

"Please, just release us," said Joe. He took another hit of the joint and passed it to Frank. "Come on. What do you want, man?"

"Actually, I could use some help," said Doctor Frownyface with a smile. "I need two able-bodied, yet simple-minded men to do my bidding."

"That's us! We could be…" said Joe. He thought for a second and snapped his fingers. "We could be your minions!"

"Ba-na-na," Frank said through a big cloud of garlicy scented marijuana smoke.

"Oh, good! I like your enthusiasm," Doctor Frownyface said and turned to his assistant. "Missy, the Super-Dopiods!"

Missy Gore sprang forward, squatted down between the two security guards and stabbed them each in the shoulders with glowing green syringes.

"Yep, this is nothing like *Saw*," Frank said through the pain.

"What?! No!!!" yelled Joe. He grasped fruitlessly for the syringe embedded, just out of reach, in his shoulder.

"I don't feel so good," Frank slurred.

The security guard's bodies tensed up and their heads rolled loosely to the side. The light in their eyes went out and was replaced by a hollow-eyed, vacant stare. Great dollops of green foam oozed from the guards' mouths. Doctor Frownyface cackled with delight.

"Now you are my Dopiod zombie slaves!" he screamed.

Missy Gore pulled the empty syringes from the guards' backs. She stood up and fixed her skirt. Doctor Frownyface laughed deeply.

"What?" Missy Gore said in a tone that showed her annoyance.

"You're standing in their pee spot," said Doctor Frownyface with a mirthful giggle.

7

The girls were all spread out around Muffy's pool in their skimpiest bikinis. Muffy and the squad splashed and swam around in the pool. Molly got out of the pool and joined Autumn and Mary Jane on the deck by the deep end as they passed a joint and sunbathed on towels.

"That smells delicious," said Molly.

Autumn passed the joint to Molly and took a big swig from a liquor bottle. Lucy got out of the pool and noticed two guys across the street in the gap between houses.

"Is that Holtie?" asked Lucy.

Holtie stood on the sidewalk and talked with Greg Scooper, one of his old friends from high school. Holtie handed Greg a bottle of pills with a frowny face on the label. Greg reached out to shake Holtie's hand and palmed some money to him.

"Hey, Holtie," yelled Muffy as she waved to Holtie from her backyard. Holtie looked around suspiciously, saw it was Muffy, and ran over to talk with her over the gate.

"Hey, Muffy," said Holtie.

"What are you doing around here?" Muffy asked. Autumn wrapped herself in a towel and joined them.

"I was just bringing some pills to one of the guys from school," Holtie explained. "You guys want any?"

Holtie held out a bottle of the little green pills, and Autumn grabbed them out of his hand.

"I need something a little stronger," said Autumn. "What are these?"

"Something new called Dopiods," said Holtie. Molly walked over to the gate in her bikini. She brushed her hair behind her ears and gave Holtie a soft smile. Holtie's eyes drifted straight to her breasts and stayed there.

"Hey, Molly," said Holtie. "How are you doing?"

"I'm really excited for the party tonight," Molly said shyly.

"Me too," said Muffy. "Hey, come swim with us!"

"I didn't bring a suit," Holtie said.

"That's okay," flirted Muffy. "You don't need one."

Muffy adjusted her tiny Bikini and showed off her curves for Holtie, then dived back into the pool to swim with the other girls. Muffy surfaced and smiled big like a starving shark at Holtie.

"I'd like to," Holtie stammered. "But I've got more people from school I need to see."

"How much do I owe you?" Autumn asked Holtie as she rattled the pills around in the bottle.

"Hey, for you guys, first one's free," Holtie said. "Do you want any, Molly?"

"No, I'll just stick to my boring old weed for now," laughed Molly.

"Okay, well, I'll see you tonight," Holtie said and jogged back to the sidewalk.

"Bye," said Molly softly, and she stared at Holtie's ass in his tight jeans the entire time he walked away down the street.

8

Mr. Smith turned on the television in the family room. He sat down on the couch next to Mrs. Smith while the three adorable but rambunctious Smith children jumped up and down on the couch and screamed their heads off. An advertisement began to play on T.V. of people, depressed and in despair, barely getting through their day.

"Sometimes life is overwhelming. Depression, anxiety, life's small annoyances," a British woman said in voiceover. "But you don't have to go it alone."

The people in the ad now grinned widely as they popped tiny green pills and frolicked through meadows of wildflowers.

"Now there are Dopiods!" the British woman said emphatically. "Still perfectly legal, you don't even need a prescription."

The people in the ad were now glassy-eyed and sat in their meadows of wildflowers, zombified and drooling. The British voiceover woman went into a motor-mouthed sprint.

"Side effects include lethargy and drooling, may be addictive. Use only as directed as overdoses may occur," the British voiceover woman said breathlessly. "Find Dopiods where you usually find your pharmaceuticals, on a street corner near you!"

The Smiths looked at the bottle of Dopiods they had purchased earlier from Nacho sitting on their coffee table next to the remote. The Smith children jumped and screamed and ran around the room.

"Dopiods!" intoned the British voiceover woman. "Make it all go away."

The Smiths exchanged glances and then both reached for the pill bottle simultaneously.

Greg Scooper clocked in for his shift at the ice cream parlor. Greg had been in his school's gifted and talented program since elementary school and had graduated with honors from his high school. Then Greg's dad, Bernie Scooper, went to jail for stock manipulation, but not before the government had seized the house and Bernie had completely drained Greg's college fund in his own legal defense. Greg's future vaporized in an instant. Now he was on his own and needed this job selling ice cream to snot-nosed brats and entitled tourists just to survive.

Greg looked at the pill bottle Holtie had given him earlier. Whatever, thought Greg, as he opened the bottle and took one of the tiny green pills.

The Smiths sat on the couch with glassy-eyed stares, drooling all over themselves while the Smith kids went crazy, hit them both in the faces with inflatable toys, and spilled cereal all over them and their new couch.

Greg Scooper stood glassy-eyed at the soft serve machine, and drooled as he made a cone. The ice cream squeezed out of the machine and spilled endlessly off the cone onto the floor. It wasn't what Greg Scooper had wanted for his life, but at this point, it was still better than being Greg Scooper.

9

The mayor's aide unzipped his pants and took his dick into her mouth. A television in the corner of Stu Paddick's messy mayoral office blared a pharmaceutical ad.

"…where you usually find your pharmaceuticals, on a street corner near you!" Said the British voiceover woman. "Dopiods! Make it all go away."

"Dopiods? I should get me some of those," said Stu as he slid deeper into his desk chair and his aide's mouth. "Hey, Candy. What time is my first meeting tomorrow? 1 p.m., right?"

Candy slobbered all over the mayor's cock and tried to speak. Without breaking stride, her mouth full of dick, Candy held up two fingers.

"Oh, 2 p.m.," said Stu. "Less teeth, sweetie. We don't have a dental plan."

Candy continued to blow the mayor but held up her middle finger to register her displeasure. The mayor chuckled to himself and watched as his underling orally pleasured his baloney pony. A nature documentary with a shark came on television, and the mayor scrambled for the remote to turn off the T.V.

"Shark! Did you see that?" shouted Stu. "I donate to all these charities, and call me galeophobic, but I would never donate to any charity that helps sharks."

Candy bobbed and sucked and rolled her eyes at the mayor.

"I hope all the sharks die," mused Stu and then came down Candy's throat with a series of staccato grunts.

10

The Dopiod-zombified security guards stood in the middle of Doctor Frownyface's makeshift laboratory. They wore scrubs and surgical masks. Doctor Frownyface laughed maniacally as Missy Gore placed paper surgical caps on the security guards' heads.

"Excellent! Do you realize what this means, Missy Gore?" chortled the mad scientist. "I, Doctor Frownyface, now possess the tools necessary to acquire the critical resources I need for my research!"

Missy Gore was unimpressed. She'd seen Frownyface at his best and at his worst. She knew what he was capable of. She knew he worked minor miracles. She knew his power. Take anything special, birthday cake maybe, and eat it every day of your life and it quits being special. It's just another birthday cake. The only thing Doctor Frownyface could possibly do that could even surprise her at this point would be to fail.

"Now, my mindless Dopiod zombies, you will obey my every command!" screamed Doctor Frownyface. "Do you understand?"

"Yes, Doctor Frownyface," Joe and Frank said in unison. Missy Gore handed Frank a speculum and Joe a wire coat hanger.

"Listen well! I need you to bring me fetuses!" hissed Doctor Frownyface through his yellow teeth.

Doctor Frownyface stepped forward and handed Joe a Shop Vac. Missy Gore handed Frank a vintage handheld Dustbuster.

"I need fresh fetuses for my work," growled Doctor Frownyface. "Do you understand?"

"Yes, Doctor Frownyface," said Frank and Joe in unison.

Doctor Frownyface stood back and threw his hands in the air with a dramatic flourish. Missy Gore facepalmed and shook her head in embarrassment.

"Now go! Go my Serial Abortionists! Bring me fresh fetuses! The fresher the better," cried the mad doctor. "Any inseminated female will do. Go! Get them by any means necessary! Do as I command you!"

Doctor Frownyface doubled over in a fit of laughter while the zombified security guards shuffled toward the door as their vacuums loudly sucked the empty air.

"We will do as you command, Doctor Frownyface. Must collect fetuses," said Joe and Frank, as they ambled out the door and off into the night.

CHAPTER 4

1

The party at the Pen15 Gang junkyard raged as Molly and her friends arrived. Fires burned in large steel drums all around the broken and smashed cars, and loud motorcycles revved and rumbled around the lot. This was a place of lawlessness and danger. The girls watched the biker bacchanal nervously as Molly pulled out her phone.

"I texted him we're here," said Molly.

Holtie had anxiously awaited Molly's text. He was really excited to see her. He stood in the middle of the junkyard with a group of laughing bikers, who cheered as Harley shotgunned a beer and smashed the can on his forehead. Holtie excused himself, stepped away and ran outside to meet the girls.

"I'm glad you guys could make it!" said Holtie with a smile as he approached Molly's car.

"Me too!" bubbled Molly.

"Hey, Holtie, where's the beer?" asked Muffy.

One of the Pen15 bikers stumbled down the street with his girlfriend and handed Autumn his beer as they wandered into the woods to have sex. Holtie jokingly bowed to the girls and pointed to the junkyard gate.

"Right this way, ladies," said Holtie.

Holtie led the girls through the rowdy crowd. A giant hairy biker in a grimy leather vest made out with a girl with red hair and face piercings just inside the gate. An older biker with a greying beard stood in the center of a group of laughing bikers and pulled out a gun. Someone threw a liquor bottle into the air and the grey beard biker shot it out of the sky. Glass particles rained down on a puddle of stagnant scum and used condoms inside a stack of old tires.

A blonde and a brunette, both in short skirts and leather jackets, sucked face and ground their pelvises together on the hood of a smashed BMW while a crowd of horny bikers cheered them on. Holtie led Molly and her friends to a keg of beer near one of the flaming barrels and started handing them red cups. Autumn downed her first beer from the biker outside and poured herself a refill from the keg.

"This is pretty crazy, Holtie," Molly shouted over the music and revelry of the crowd.

"It's like this most nights. Hey, let's go find someplace to sit," said Holtie as he took a sip of his beer.

Holtie led them toward a quieter spot in the junkyard. The biker with the handlebar mustache and the biker with the scruffy beard were kissing on the hood of a totaled Ferrari while a crowd of biker chicks cheered them on. A biker with a tattoo of a tiger on his face stuck a needle into his arm and shot up next to an unconscious girl wearing a bikini top, Daisy Dukes, and a cowboy hat. Next to them, two girls in their underwear shotgunned a joint and felt each other up.

Muffy nudged Molly and pointed at a couple furiously fucking on the roof of a rusty red jeep while the Pen15 Gang watched. A circle of glassy-eyed bikers had formed around a flaming steel drum. A heavily tattooed biker took a little green pill and kneeled down next to a drooling girl in leather pants and a heavy metal T-shirt. The biker's eyes glassed over and he began to drool as the Dopiods flowed freely through his system. Holtie nodded a greeting to Jake. Jake waved a hello, then popped several Dopiods into his mouth, and walked over to kneel down in the middle of the Dopiod circle.

A big, fat biker with a goatee sat on a stack of tires on the edge of the circle. He smoked a fat blunt and watched the drooling bikers, while a tiny girl with green hair, tattoos, and pigtails sucked his dick. He took a long drag and passed the blunt to the girl. She stopped blowing him to smoke, handed the blunt back and returned to sucking his cock. Holtie and the squad stopped to watch, and the green-haired pigtail girl looked up with the biker's thick throbbing member still in her mouth and winked at Holtie.

Jake's body began to twitch in the center of the

encircled Dopiod zombies. An acid yellow foam poured from Jake's lips and his jaw went slack. A few bikers from the crowd noticed and pointed when Jake fell over writhing, but only Holtie recognized that Jake was having an overdose.

"Hold on. I'll be right back," Holtie said to Molly as he dashed to where Jake lay crumpled and convulsing.

The girls watched in horror as Jake's head wobbled around and his tongue lashed more yellow froth down the front of his shirt. Holtie grabbed Jake by the collar, shook him, and tried to revive him with a few firm pats on his cheeks. The crowd recoiled at the sudden chaos and grew silent.

"Nacho! Harley!," yelled Holtie. "I think Jake is overdosing!"

Nacho and a biker with a shaved head picked up Jake's exhausted, quivering body and began to drag him from the ring of Dopiod zombies. A hushed pall fell over the Pen15 Gang. Harley shoved his way through the crowd into the center of the circle, his face a mask of rage that glowed red in the light of the smoldering fires in the burning barrels.

"What the fuck?" yelled Harley.

"I think it's the Dopiods," said Holtie.

"Take him out back and get him some water or something, man," Harley snapped.

The silent crowd of bikers parted as Nacho and the bald biker dragged Jake's trembling body into the night.

"Hey, who said this party was over? Huh?" hollered Harley to the gawking biker horde. "I'm still wanting to have a good time!"

The Pen15 Gang members look around at each other, not sure what to do next. They had been having just as much fun as Harley but watching Jake overdose had suddenly cast a gloom over the celebration. The bikers began to party again, but in a much more reserved manner than they had before. Molly looked shaken as Holtie returned. Autumn saw Molly wasn't drinking her beer, so she snatched Molly's red solo cup and downed the suds in one gulp.

"Sorry about that," said Holtie as he looked nervously around at the girls.

"What was that all about?" asked Muffy.

"Nothing," lied Holtie, as the icy rush of adrenaline still chilled his veins. "Jake? He just had a little too much."

"Too much of what?" asked Muffy.

Molly looked around at her friends. A few confident bikers had come over to flirt with Addy, Autumn, and Lucy. Mary Jane and Poppers had also broken away and grooved to the music and grinded against each other to the delight of the crowd. Muffy was still drooling over Holtie. Molly suddenly felt very out of place, and a strong desire to leave crept over her.

"Hey, I'm still good to drive, and I think we should probably get going after that," Molly said seriously. She looked around at her friends as they had fun and danced with the Pen15 bikers. She saw Autumn grab two more beers from a passing biker and begin to chug them. But Molly had seen enough for one night.

"I get it. I guess things kind of went downhill there," said Holtie as he sensed Molly's unease. "Hey, maybe you guys can come over to my place, well, my Mom's place? She usually goes out weekends, so I have the place to myself."

"Yes, please," said Muffy.

"We have beer," said Holtie. "And I have weed."

"That sounds like fun," Molly said and relaxed a little bit as Holtie tried to take control of the situation. Autumn, who had been listening in, finished one of her beers and danced over to Molly, Muffy, and Holtie.

"I think we're going to stay, you guys. There are a lot of cute guys and I'm still having fun," said Autumn. The rest of the squad raised their beers and cheered with excitement as the group of leering bikers around them grew bigger.

"Call me if you need anything," Molly said to Autumn.

"I think I'll be fine," said Autumn as she chugged the last of her beer and jumped on a tan, tattoo-covered biker.

"So, I guess it's just the three of us then?" said Muffy, caressing Holtie's chest as she walked away from the party. Holtie and Molly exchanged concerned glances and followed her through the growing biker orgy, to the junkyard gate, and out to Molly's car.

Molly, Muffy, and Holtie drove off into the night as Autumn stumbled out of the junkyard.

2

The tattooed biker she clung to stuck his hand down the back of her pants and squeezed a generous handful of ass. He shoved his hand deeper and stroked her labia through her damp panties with his rough fingers. Autumn grinned, took a deep swig from a flask and kissed the biker hard on the lips.

"I'm pregnant so we don't need a condom," said Autumn as she unbuttoned her pants, making just enough room for the biker to slip a finger inside of her. "But let me go pee first, because I'm not into that shit."

Autumn wriggled free from the biker's clutches and ambled away from the loud party into the nearby woods. Her shoes were perfect for partying but impractical for hiking. She spotted a large bush that she could hide behind and stumbled deeper into the trees.

Two pairs of eyes watched her from the darkness as she partially slipped on the thick, wet leaf mulch and grabbed a tree trunk for support. Autumn pulled down her pants and panties together in one quick move and squatted behind the bush. She eased her pants down a little more as a stream of hot piss sizzled into a puddle in the dirt.

The Serial Abortionists sprang from the inky blankness with their vacuum cleaners and clothes hangers, and caught Autumn with her pants down.

They pushed her face first into the wet ground and held her before she could even react.

"No! Please!" Autumn gasped into a musty pile of leaves. "What are you doing!"

The Serial Abortionist previously known as Joe held his hand firmly on Autumn's shoulders, pressing her face hard into the ground. She tried to kick at her two attackers, but the pants around her knees restricted her movement.

"Help!" Autumn tried breathlessly to yell and groaned instead from the weight of Joe's hand pushing down on her shoulder blades. The Serial Abortionist previously known as Frank pulled the speculum from the pocket of his scrubs and shoved the cold metal instrument into Autumn's vagina and squeezed the device to expose her cervix. Serial Abortionist Joe held his vacuum hose with crevice attachment at the ready.

"No! Stop!" Autumn cried, trying to straighten out her legs and fight against the assault of the bent clothes hanger as it entered her. "Please don't abort my baby!"

Serial Abortionist Joe turned on the vacuum and handed the hose to Serial Abortionist Frank, who shoved it deep into Autumn's womb. Autumn struggled in vain and cried into the pile of leaves.

"Don't abort my baby," was the last thing Autumn said before she blacked out, perhaps from the terror or perhaps from the alcohol. A sickening slurping sound emanated from the vacuum hose and the fetus hit the bottom of the shop vac with a thunk. Serial Abortionist

Joe emotionlessly turned off the vacuum and deposited the harvested fetus into a fluid filled collection jar with a splash. The deed done, the Serial Abortionists fled back into the darkness, leaving the unconscious Autumn alone in a puddle of urine and blood beneath the bush.

3

"Okay, keep quiet for just a second," whispered Holtie to Muffy and Molly. Holtie carefully opened the door and looked around the kitchen. His mother sat on a kitchen stool and snored over a pile of pharmaceutical pill bottles and a bottle of vodka, as she lay her head on the counter.

"My mom's asleep," he said. "Follow me."

Holtie quietly led the girls into the kitchen and past the sleeping Karen. He stopped at the fridge to grab a 6-pack of beer and snuck Molly and Muffy upstairs to his bedroom on the other side of the house. Holtie entered the bedroom and flipped the glowing red switch on a power strip, which turned on a string of Christmas lights strung across his room. The walls of Holtie's bedroom were festooned with motorcycle and biker posters, and another string of purple lights were draped over the headboard of the bed.

"You guys can smoke in here," Holtie said as he ushered the girls inside. He handed them beers and pulled out an ashtray, a tray of weed, and a bong from the stand beside his bed. Molly picked up a joint from the tray and lit it, while Muffy looked at pictures of Holtie playing sports in middle school that hung on a cork board in the dim light of the twinkling Christmas lights.

"Oh, you were cute even back then," said Muffy.

"Yeah, I used to be big into football," said Holtie.

"That explains all the muscles," Muffy said with a grin and ran her fingers down Holtie's stomach. Molly sat on the bed, opened her beer, and blew marijuana smoke towards the purple lights over the bed. Holtie stretched out on the bed beside her. Muffy opened her beer and took a big drink as she watched Molly and Holtie.

"So what do you guys want to do?" asked Holtie.

"I guess we could watch some T.V.," said Molly.

Holtie reached over Molly to grab the remote. Molly breathed in his cologne and felt the heat radiating from his hard stomach as it brushed against her chest. Holtie flicked on the T.V. and switched from the cartoon channel to a band performing on a late night talk show. Muffy kicked off her shoes and sat down on the bed on the other side of Holtie.

The band finished its set and the late night talk show ended. Images of Mayor Stu Paddick opening the beach, followed by archival footage of a river shark flashed across the television as a news report from Newsman Wes Chestleydale began.

"Tonight at 11… A local man's arm is missing after an apparent shark attack at Riverside Beach," said

Newsman Wes Chestleydale from the glowing T.V. screen. "If confirmed, this would indicate a return of river sharks to our area and would be the seventeenth river shark attack in the last five years. City officials have yet to be reached for comment. Stay tuned for our continuing coverage. And tune in tomorrow night when we'll have more of my special report on a new drug called Dopiods."

Suddenly a clip of Doctor Frownyface, disguised in a wig, fake mustache and stethoscope, appeared on the screen.

"To answer your questions, yes, Dopiods are completely safe," said the disguised Doctor Frownyface. "When used as directed, or otherwise."

"This has been your local news update. I'm Wes Chestleydale," said Newsman Wes Chestleydale with a smile. "Now, please stay tuned for more late night programming."

Muffy, who had watched Holtie and Molly closely, decided to make her move.

"I know something else we can do," Muffy said, as she took off her shirt, climbed on top of Holtie and straddled his waist.

Molly's eyes got big as she took a hit of the joint and immediately had a coughing fit. Holtie turned from Muffy to Molly with a look of pure shock on his face. Molly tried to shake the cough and passed the joint to Holtie, who then took a big hit and stared in total disbelief at Muffy's luscious melons as she reached behind her back and undid her bra.

"Whoa. I mean, are you sure?" Holtie stammered. "Are both of you into that?"

"Molly thinks you're cute, Holtie," Muffy said as she freed her tan round breasts and tossed her bra off the bed. "She does"t mind, do you, Molly?"

"I think you're kind of cute," Molly managed to squeak.

Molly looked hard into Holtie's eyes. Holtie looked from Muffy's breasts to Molly, then leaned over to Molly, put his hand on her face, drew her in, and kissed her deeply on the mouth. Muffy bit her lip as she watched the two kissing. Without breaking her gaze, Muffy reached down and yanked at Holtie's belt. She pushed his shirt up on his stomach and felt his abs ripple against her hands as she seized the front of his jeans and undid the button.

Holtie's rock hard cock strained against his pants leg as Muffy unzipped his jeans and kissed his stomach between his boxers and belly button. Holtie got goosebumps and closed his eyes. He sucked tenderly on Molly's lower lip, then gasped as Muffy gently kissed towards his pelvis.

"Mmmmm," Muffy moaned hungrily as she felt his thick dick through the denim.

Muffy yanked at Holtie's jeans and pulled his rigid member over the top of his boxers. Holtie gasped again as Muffy licked beneath the head of his penis, blew softly along the shaft, and took the tip between her lips and teeth. Opening her mouth wider to accommodate his girth, Muffy tasted a small squirt of Holtie's pre-cum on her tongue. Holtie and Molly stopped kissing and they both watched as Muffy's quivering lips enthusiastically sucked Holtie's dick.

Muffy pulled up the front of her skirt so Molly could watch Holtie's thick, veiny cock slide deep into the silky smoothness of her freshly waxed pussy. Holtie handed the joint to Muffy and reached behind Molly's back to undo her bra. Muffy took a few drags on the joint, carefully dismounted, and reached over to ash in the ashtray. Then Molly got on all fours in front of Holtie and reached between his legs, stroking his dick with an amateur's fascination. She'd never seen one this big before.

Molly rolled onto her back and pulled off her shorts and panties. Holtie spit into his hand and stroked his cock. Muffy took another puff on the joint and shotgunned it to Holtie, who exhaled the thin cloud of smoke toward the purple Christmas lights. Muffy put the joint in the ashtray and rubbed her clit, then reached down and guided Holtie's big dick inside Molly. Holtie reached a hand up Muffy's skirt and shoved two fingers deep inside her vagina.

Holtie lay on his back while Molly rode him and he thrusted his rock hard dick balls deep inside her. Molly felt him hitting the back of her vagina with an uncomfortable aching throb. It hurt so bad but it hurt so good. Muffy sat on Holtie's face and watched Molly fuck Holtie as he licked and sucked her smooth lips and clit to climax. Muffy's legs shook and she squirted a little in Holtie's mouth and down his chin and chest.

Holtie swallowed and gasped for air as Muffy crawled off the bed satisfied. Holtie grabbed Molly by the hair, guided her off him onto all fours on the bed and began to fuck her doggystyle from behind. Holtie wrapped Molly's hair around his fist and pulled her head back, while Muffy fired up the bong, took a big rip and watched.

"Oh God! Oh God! Oh God!" cried Molly with each piston thrust Holtie made inside her from behind. Holtie pulled Molly's hair again and shoved her face into a pillow. With one hand Molly played with her nipples. She reached the other hand between her legs and rapidly flicked her fingers back and forth across her swollen clit.

Muffy pulled a thin black leather harness and hot pink dildo from her purse and slipped it on over her legs. She tightened the straps against her thighs, smacked her ass, and hopped on the bed behind Holtie. Muffy spit on the strap-on and worked it until it glistened. Muffy held open Holtie's ass as he thrust hard inside Molly and then guided the wet dildo into his butthole. Sandwiched between the girls, Holtie's eyes grew huge as Muffy thrust the dildo deep inside his unprepared ass.

"Still tender back there!" grunted Holtie, going

cross-eyed from the cold fullness that pressed against his prostate as Molly and Muffy both moaned and bucked hard against him.

Muffy pumped the strap-on hard up Holtie's ass until he came harder than he ever had in his life. With a loud moan, Holtie pulled out of Molly and shot hot cum onto her face and chest. His legs shook as Muffy finished butt fucking him and pulled out. Holtie squeezed a big glob of pearly ejaculate onto Molly's clit and shoved the tip of his throbbing meat missile back inside Molly's slit. Molly's eyes rolled into the back of her head as she rubbed her cum-covered clit to completion.

"Mmm. Yes! Give it to me, daddy! Give me that cum! Fuck! Yes!" cried Molly.

Holtie wiped his dick on his comforter and wriggled beneath the sheets. Molly plucked the half smoked joint out of the ashtray and fired it back up. Muffy climbed under the sheets and draped her naked leg over Holtie as his dick throbbed and bounced against the back of her knee.

"Well, that was fun," said Muffy as she lit a cigarette. She took a puff and passed it to Holtie.

"Yeah," said Holtie, totally fucked out.

Muffy kissed Holtie on the lips and ran her nails along his muscly chest, across his stomach and down through his treasure trail. Holtie shuddered and handed the cigarette back to Muffy as she got out of bed naked, stretched, and started to look around the room for her clothes.

"You were great, Holtie," said Molly as she handed the joint to Holtie, and joined Muffy in the nude search for clothing.

"Yeah?" Holtie said as he blissfully watched the two naked girls scamper and jiggle around his room while he chilled in bed. "Yeah."

"Okay, well, we'd better get going," said Muffy.

"Yeah? Okay, yeah," Holtie said, in a moment of post nut clarity. "Make sure my mom is sleeping and I'll sneak you out."

"It's okay. We'll just show ourselves out," Muffy said, adjusting her skirt. "Come on, Molly."

"I had fun tonight, Holtie," Molly said as she put on her shirt and shoved her bra into her purse. "We should do it again sometime."

Muffy put the strap-on back into her purse, picked up her shoes, and headed out the door. Molly leaned over Holtie, her hand resting on his blanket-covered thigh. Holtie felt the cum sticking the sheets to his leg as Molly kissed him longingly on the lips. Then she picked up her shoes and ran out the door after Muffy.

"Yeah? Okay, yeah. Sure. Yeah." said Holtie to the empty room. Literally and figuratively drained, he slowly drifted off to sleep.

CHAPTER 5

1

Holtie woke to the sound of a text notification on his phone, a sunbeam in his eye, and dried cum that had glued his sheets to his leg hair. Holtie unstuck himself from the sheet and put on his boxers. *Meet me at the mall in 30*, Harley had written. Holtie slid into his jeans and found a fresh t-shirt in his dresser drawer. He grabbed his jacket and the keys to his bike and rushed out the door to meet Harley.

"I got lavender detergent, like you said, and I love it. Very calming," said Karen into a cordless landline telephone as she emptied the contents of her laundry basket into the washing machine. "I just get so stressed out. I don't know why."

Karen carried the empty laundry basket upstairs to Holtie's room and began to pick the dirty clothes up off the floor. She winced at the sour smell radiating from a pair of her son's sweat socks and used a pen from Holtie's desk to pick up his underwear.

"I'm just so worried about Holtie. He's just not motivated," Karen said as she shook her head at Holtie's unmade bed. "And he's been extra moody recently. The other night he stormed out and didn't come home."

Karen pulled back the cum crusted comforter and found a tiny pair of thong underwear between the sheets.

"I know, Cheryl. Well, it looks like he must have been home last night. His bed isn't made," said Karen, disgusted. "And it looks like he must have had a girl here."

Karen pursed her lips in disappointment as she picked up the empty beer cans and emptied his ashtray into the garbage. Then her eyes fell on the tray of weed and a bong barely concealed on the floor beside Holtie's bed. Her jaw dropped.

"Listen, Cheryl, I need to call you back," Karen said and hung up the phone and set it upon Holtie's desk, next to the bag of Dopiod pill bottles. Karen picked up the bottle and carefully studied the label.

"These pills aren't from our doctor," Karen said. She sat on the end of Holtie's bed and examined the frowny face symbol on the pill bottle.

2

Molly was fresh out of the shower, wearing only a robe, when her phone rang. She checked the hallway to make sure Stu wasn't spying on her, then Molly sprinted to her bedroom.

"Oh, hey, Autumn!" Molly said into the phone. "How was the rest of the party last night?"

"Molly, I had an abortion," said Autumn.

"Oh, Autumn. It's for the best. I think you made the right choice," Molly said, sympathetically.

Autumn wore a silky nightie as she sat on the floor of her bathroom and clutched her phone. She had been crying and her makeup was smeared.

"It wasn't my choice, Molly," said Autumn as a tear ran down her cheek.

"I don't understand," said Molly and pulled her robe tight around herself.

"These two guys… I was peeing in the woods… Clothes hanger and vacuums…" Autumn sniffed into the phone. "They aborted my baby, Molly. They aborted… They borted baby. Borted… Bababy…"

"Autumn, are you alright? Are you on Dopiods or something?" Molly said.

"I think I took too many. Help me, Molly," Autumn said weakly. "Help me… Helbe Melbie…"

Autumn's head rolled to the side. Her eyes glassed over and the lights began to go out. Her arm fell limp and she dropped the phone on the bathroom floor.

"Autumn! Oh god! Autumn, are you still there?" Molly cried. "Autumn?!?"

Autumn began to writhe and twitch. She choked as a yellow foam poured from her mouth and she fell over onto the bathroom floor with her face next to the phone. Molly could hear Autumn's labored breathing through the receiver and she began to cry hysterically, helpless to do anything while her friend gurgled and died on the phone.

"Autumn! No! Autumn! Don't die," screamed Molly. "Please, don't die! Autumn! No!!!"

3

Harley and Nacho stood outside a women's clothing store at the mall when Holtie walked up. Holtie nodded and they nodded back.

"How's Jake?" asked Holtie.

"Oh, man, Jake died," said Nacho, morosely. "Overdose, man."

"What?" Holtie said in disbelief.

"That's just the way it goes sometimes," said Harley as he shifted from foot to foot and looked nervous.

"These new Dopiods seem dangerous," said Holtie.

"Hey, I don't know," said Harley with a look over his shoulders. "They sure make stealing shit easier. Watch the door for me."

Harley pulled a pistol out of his pants and moved quickly into the clothing store, followed by Nacho.

Holtie looked around the nearly empty mall and a surge of confused adrenaline propelled him to follow. A glassy-eyed clothing store clerk drooled at the register in the middle of the store. The clerk was so high on Dopiods that she didn't even flinch when Harley ran in and fired his gun in the air.

"Listen up, everybody! This is a robbery!" yelled Harley as several topless women ran from the dressing rooms and out into the mall at the sound of gunfire.

"Mall shooter!" screamed a pregnant shopper, who clutched her face in terror and fled.

"Come on, Harley," said Holtie as he nervously kept an eye on the door out to the mall.

Harley spun around and erratically pointed the gun toward anything that moved. Nacho ran to the register and grabbed a bag. The zombified store clerk put up no resistance as Nacho emptied all the bills from the register into the bag. Nacho grabbed several rolls of coins and then ran for the door. Holtie frantically followed him out. Harley aimed the gun at the out-to-lunch store clerk as he backed towards the door.

"Bang," said Harley, as he put the gun back in the back of his pants.

"Stop thieves," lisped a fat kid in a fukumen-zukin ninja mask and hood. He held a katana sword sideways at eye level. Harley froze in his tracks as several more Mall Ninjas emerged. A gangly Mall Ninja in a camouflage gaiter and spiked arm braces stepped out from behind an ornamental planter and swung a grappling hook on a long black cord. Another Mall Ninja with a long black ponytail, wraparound sunglasses, and cargo pants flicked his wrists to reveal two spring-loaded arm blades. A pasty Mall Ninja with a neckbeard and a sweatband unsheathed a gold dragon-shaped knife from a rhinestone encrusted scabbard.

"Damn!" swore Harley. "Mall Ninjas!"

Nacho sized-up the gangly Mall Ninja with the grappling hook and swung the bag of stolen money at his head. The rolls of coins smacked the Mall Ninja square in the face and broke his nose with a sickening thwack. Blood spilled from the Mall Ninja's camo gaiter and down his Brony t-shirt.

A hidden Mall Ninja peaked out from behind a garbage can and tossed several throwing stars in Holtie's direction. The throwing stars missed Holtie, hit a pillar, and clattered worthlessly to the sparkle-flecked mall floor.

Harley reached for his gun, but it had slid out of his waistband, down into his underwear and deep into the crack of his ass. In frustration, Harley let out a primal cry and charged the pasty Mall Ninja with the dragon knife. Harley barely dodged the Mall Ninja's knife and punched as hard as he could. He hit the sickly kid's chest with enough force to bust his rib cage open. Blood exploded from the Mall Ninja's chest as Harley seized his still beating heart and ripped it from his chest.

The fat, lispy Mall Ninja swung his katana in a figure eight motion and advanced on Holtie. Holtie ducked out of the way as the blade sliced through an ornamental mall plant with ease. The fat Mall Ninja advanced again and swung wildly at Holtie, but missed by mere inches. Holtie backed away terrified.

The cargo pants Mall Ninja with the ponytail uncrossed his arms and pinwheeled towards Nacho. Nacho screamed as the Mall Ninja's arm blades tore through his throat. Nacho gagged and fell to his knees as blood spurted from the gaping wound in his thick tattooed neck.

The fat Mall Ninja brandished his sword in the air and growled with rage as he ran at Holtie. His foot slid in the growing puddle of blood on the floor and his sword crashed through a mall directory sign. Holtie pounced at the opportunity and punched the fat Mall Ninja directly in the face, which knocked him unconscious. Holtie grabbed the sword from the smashed mall directory sign and looked around in panic.

Harley was covered in blood and fought off several Mall Ninjas in the middle of a tile fountain. Nacho lay on the floor and grasped at his throat. His eyes bulged as fresh hot blood poured from his mouth. In the distance, Holtie could hear police sirens as they closed in. Holtie left Harley, Nacho, and his bike behind as he ran as fast as he could from the mall.

4

Mayor Stu Paddick walked out of City Hall toward an awaiting limo. A throng of reporters chased after him.

"She was 18! No, 19! I swear. Whatever she told you I have a full alibi. No, two alibis!" Paddick said, walking briskly from the swarm of reporters. "I will not stand here idly and be slandered. I am completely innocent and this was a setup. Witch hunt! False flag! Fake news!"

"Um… Mayor Paddick, do you have any comments on the recent overdoses?" a reporter in a fedora yelled from the mob of media.

"What? Who said I can't handle my own?" the Mayor scoffed. "Sure, I may get a little hungover at times, but I'd hardly consider that an overdose."

"The DOPIOD overdoses, Mr. Mayor?" the reporter in the fedora said, in a fruitless attempt at a follow-up question.

"Hey, fellas. You have a nice day, okay," Mayor Paddick said as he zig-zagged toward the limo. "Sorry to disappoint, but there is no story here."

"Mr. Mayor, what do you intend to do about Dopiods," tried a reporter in a tweed jacket. The chauffeur of the limo, a woman in a jacket, a driving hat, and a fake mustache, opened the door of the awaiting limo upon the Mayor's approach.

"Great weather we're having, huh? Not a shark seen

for miles," said Paddick, beginning to get into the limo. The faux chauffeur walked to the driver's seat. The scrum of stringers slung more questions in the mayor's direction before he could slam the limo door.

"Mayor Paddick!" yelled the reporter in the fedora.

"Do you think Dopiods are responsible for the overdoses?" said Newsman Wes Chestleydale as he thrusted a microphone in the Mayor's face. "And who is responsible for the Dopiods?"

"I want all the citizens of our fair city to know I'm always working for them and I'll be holding a press conference in my office later today," said the mayor, who dodged the questions with a wave of his hand. "Now, if you'll excuse me. I've got some official mayor's business to attend to, so…"

The mayor slammed the limo door shut, closed his eyes and rubbed his temples. Missy Gore removed the fake mustache and chauffeur hat and pulled away from the curb. The mayor shook his head, sat back and opened his eyes. Doctor Frownyface sat directly across from him, a manilla envelope clutched in his thick black rubber gloves.

"Okay, now what the fuck are you?" asked Paddick.

"My name is Doctor Frownyface, and I want you to ignore this Dopiod crisis and do exactly as I say," said Doctor Frownyface with a toothy yellow smile.

"Well, it's like they told me when I bought my way into USC," said Stu. "Ignorance is expensive. And with my grade point average, I'd have to do more than donate a new library."

"I don't think you understand. You are going to do exactly as I say, and you are going to do it for nothing," said Doctor Frownyface.

"Oh, yeah," said the Mayor defiantly. "And why the fuck would I do that?"

Doctor Frownyface tossed the manilla envelope to the mayor, who opened it and pulled out several black and white photos. Photos of Mayor Paddick, dressed in drag, hanging out in a dark alley with Lady Midnight and Ms. Carmelita, the two drag queen prostitutes.

"Okay, well, I think we can probably come to some sort of agreement not to release these photos of me," Mayor Paddick said abruptly. "What did you say your demands were?"

Stu flipped through the photos and found one he really liked. He removed the photo from the stack, folded it, and stuck it into his pocket.

"Doc, you may be a lowlife blackmailer," said the mayor, "but you are a damn good photographer."

5

Molly, Muffy, and the rest of the girls watched as a stretcher with a body bag was wheeled out of Autumn's apartment and through the lines responding police cars and fire trucks to the awaiting ambulance.

"I can't believe Autumn is dead," said Molly.

"And we were supposed to go to the river today," Muffy said and shook her head. "They said it looked like a suicide. She seemed fine yesterday. I wonder what she didn't tell us."

"I don't know anything," said Molly, her arms insecurely crossed over her chest. "I'll see you guys later."

Molly walked away down the street toward her car.

"Molly!" Holtie said from his hiding place in a nearby bush. "I am so glad to see you."

"Holtie, what's the matter?" said Molly and stepped behind the bush where Holtie hid.

"I saw all the cops, and…" said Holtie, who trailed off as he peeked through the bushes to where the red and blue hazard lights of the emergency vehicles flashed.

"Holtie, Autumn is dead," said Molly.

"What?" Are you okay?" said Holtie.

"I'm fine. She was going through some… stuff," said Molly, in an attempt to change the subject. "What did you do?"

"Nothing. But I need to keep a low profile. I think the police are after me," said Holtie as he hung his head in frustration. "I didn't know anything was going to happen. Then there was this robbery."

"Why do you have a sword?" asked Molly.

"Mall Ninjas, Molly," said Holtie, with a faraway distant look in his eyes.

"Oh my god, I'm so sorry," said Molly. Her hand went to her mouth in shock. "You can hang out at my place until things cool down. Get in."

Molly unlocked her car and climbed behind the wheel. Holtie scuttled from the bushes to the passenger seat. Molly did a U-turn away from the police, and they drove off down the street.

CHAPTER 6

1

Mayor Stu Paddick was holding a press conference in the press room at City Hall. He wore a jacket over a t-shirt with his face on it that read "I'm the MAYOR, bitch!" in big letters. His aides, Ginger and Candy, wore skimpy patriotic outfits. Young protesters milled about in the back of the room and held homemade signs that said "Stop The Dopiod Crisis". A small audience had gathered as Paddick took the podium and reporters peppered him with questions.

"Mayor Paddick, what do you intend to do about the serial abortions, biker gangs, and increasing crime?" Newsman Wes Chestleydale said, aiming his microphone at Mayor Paddick.

"What do you plan to do about Dopiods?" asked the reporter in the fedora.

"Mr. Mayor! The river sharks are back. Do you have a comment?" yelled the reporter in the tweed jacket.

"Hey, thanks for coming everybody," said Paddick.

"I'm sure I can soft-shoe around all of your questions, but as I actually intend to do nothing of consequence about these problems, first I'd like to read a prepared statement full of references to patriotism, America, and freedom."

Karen Thump shoved past the protesters and into the room.

"I want to know what City Hall plans to do about the town's most pressing issue..." Karen bellowed. "Marijuana!"

"Right! Yes! Marijuana!" crowed the mayor, upon realization that this interruption was very much to his advantage. "What is your name, citizen?"

Karen pushed her way through the audience to the podium.

"Karen," she said.

"Karen, I should have known," said Mayor Paddick. "Please let everyone know what it is that's bothering you, Karen."

"Karen Thump. My name is Karen Thump, and I am outraged. Marijuana leads to biker gangs, abortions, and crime. My son used marijuana and he had premarital sex," said Karen as she held the podium and clutched her pearls. "And now, I even found Dopiod pills in his room. All because of marijuana."

"You're so right, Karen. Isn't she right, ladies and gentlemen?" said Stu as he smiled for the cameras. "Thank God for the Karens of the world."

A few people in the audience politely clapped at

that. Mayor Paddick tried to escort Karen off the stage, but she reached out and seized the podium microphone.

"I demand an immediate crackdown on marijuana," Karen shouted as her voice screeched through the loudspeaker.

"It's clear to me that the root of all our problems is marijuana! Damn reeferheads, weedeaters, hippie-hoppies. The youth element is out of control!" the mayor hollered. "An acquaintance of my step-daughter died from a Dopiod overdose, and the police tell me her system tested positive for marijuana! I tell you, it's blunt trauma!"

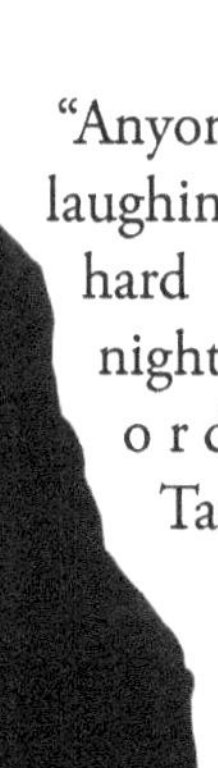

"Marijuana is to blame!" cried Karen.

"So today, I, Mayor Stu Paddick, am calling for a crackdown on marijuana users! Anyone caught using and abusing the wacky tobaccy will have their devil's lettuce confiscated."

"I demand more!" trilled Karen.

"Anyone caught laughing too hard at late night T.V., ordering Taco Bell past 10 p.m., or listening to jazz…" continued the mayor.

"More!" shrieked Karen as she nodded emphatically.

"I'm launching a… citywide abstinence program!" exclaimed the mayor.

"Good!" yelled Karen. "More!"

"And I'm recommending everyone in town buy a gun!" cheered Paddick.

"Wait. What?" said Karen.

"We will face this crisis together. Thoughts and prayers, everybody," barked the mayor. "God bless America! Now lock and load!"

The mayor clapped loudly for himself and waved to the crowd. Ginger stepped forward with a camera, and the mayor posed for several pictures behind the podium with a confused looking Karen. Candy jiggled, clapped loudly, and jumped up and down in support of the mayor's plan. The small audience again clapped politely with confused looks on their faces.

2

Things had gotten bad around town. With no efforts made to stop them, the Pen15 Gang now brazenly sold Dopiods right out in the open. And they sold them everywhere, to anyone. The police, thanks to Mayor Paddick's diversionary proclamations, had focused their attention elsewhere.

A cop car trolled the edge of the river in the

darkness of night and searched for clouds of smoke in the moonlight. Mary Jane and Addy passed a joint and laughed with some boys they had met at the river that day. The police flashed their lights and aimed a spotlight toward the group of happy stoners.

"Stop smoking the reefer, you dope fiends!" blared the police car's loud speaker. "You're all under arrest!"

Ms. Carmelita and her John sat on a bed, glassy-eyed and drooling. Lady Midnight sat down between them, popped a Dopiod pill into her mouth, and washed it down with a diet soda. Within moments, her shoulders loosened, her jaw went slack, and a string of drool fell from her lips.

The hot yoga instructor had purchased his Dopiods from a Pen15 biker directly outside his studio. Lucy and Poppers stretched on their yoga mats as the yoga instructor silently sat hunched over on the floor and drooled into his mat. Poppers looked at his lazy, faraway stare and tried to do exactly as he was doing. She made an ahegao face and stuck her tongue out while Lucy gave her a side eye.

The reporter in the fedora reclined face up on a massage table in a massage parlor while he got a rub and tug hand job. The massage girl, a cute, petite woman named Goo Dong, loosely held the reporter's erection in her motionless hand beneath a towel. Her eyes were glossed over and spit poured from her mouth onto the towel. The reporter sat up and looked quizzically from Goo Dong's glassy-eyed expression to his erection. Needless to say, he had a very unhappy ending.

The Smiths overdosed on Dopiods at home and twitched on their couch while an acid yellow foam poured from their mouths. One of the Smith children thought they were just being silly and repeatedly hit Mr. Smith in the face with a plastic bat, to no response. Another Smith child found the open Dopiod bottle with the frowny face symbol and unsupervised, popped several of the colorful green pills into his mouth.

Waitress Brandy stood in the alley behind the club on her break and smoked a joint. New hire Poindexter watched Brandy from a window as he called the police tip line. Sam the bartender stood at the bar, glassy-eyed and drooling, while he endlessly poured beer into a beer glass that overflowed uncontrollably onto the counter and down to the floor.

"Hello, police?" whispered Poindexter into the phone. "I'd like to report a pot-smoking stoner."

Moments later, the alley behind the club was illuminated by the harsh red and blue lights of a squad car.

"Put the dank chronic down, you filthy marijuana addict!" a cop crackled through the loudspeaker. "You're going to jail."

Greg Scooper had finished a double shift at the ice cream shop only an hour before. Now, he held a Dopiod bottle in his shaking hands and spilled pills all over his kitchen floor. He twitched and shook violently as an acid yellow foam poured from his mouth. It might satisfy the reader to know that Greg had always assumed his last meal would be ice cream. And it was.

3

A pregnant shopper made her way through the mall to the clothing store. She had tried to make a return to the clothing store the day before, but there had been a robbery. Three people had been killed. But with only a day left to make her return, per store policy, the pregnant shopper would not be deterred.

She finished her blue raspberry slushie and deposited the cup in a trash can. Two Mall Ninjas sat glassy-eyed while they drooled over their weapons next to the garbage can. Strangely enough, the Mall Ninjas did not have any Dopiods in their systems. The pregnant shopper recoiled in disgust, then turned and made her way to a long hallway that led to the mall bathroom.

The Serial Abortionists had stalked the pregnant women of the town all day, and they struck at random and without mercy. Their collection jar swam with fetuses. And they now silently followed the pregnant shopper down the corridor to the bathroom.

The pregnant shopper looked over her shoulder, saw the two men with their clothes hanger, speculum, and vacuums, and knew who they were. She had heard about them on the news from Newsman Wes Chestleydale. The pregnant shopper screamed and bolted down the hallway to the bathroom with the Serial Abortionists in hot pursuit.

"Help! Serial abortionists! They're going to abort

my baby!" she cried as she ran as fast as she could into the empty women's bathroom.

The Serial Abortionists ran in after her and turned on their vacuums. All the stall doors were closed, but they located the pregnant shopper with little trouble by the whimpers coming from beneath the handicapped stall. Serial Abortionist Joe kicked in the stall door.

"No! No!!! Please don't hurt me! Please, don't abort my baby! No!!!" screamed the terrified pregnant shopper.

Serial Abortionist Joe pulled out the speculum. The pregnant shopper backed into the wall and tried to crouch behind the toilet. She swung her purse, but Serial Abortionist Frank reached for her hands and held her firm. The pregnant shopper screamed and cried as the speculum was inserted into her vagina, and Serial Abortionist Frank handed over the clothes hanger. Rivulets of blood trickled from the until-then pregnant woman's legs and covered the bathroom floor.

"Help!!! No!!!" screamed the once pregnant shopper. "Help! Don't abort my baby!"

But the deed had been done. The ex-pregnant shopper cried as the dead fetus that would have been her baby girl, was vacuumed up and dumped into the sickly blue goo of the Serial Abortionists' collection jar. The Serial Abortionists fled the mall and returned to the old industrial building with their vacuums and fetuses.

Doctor Frownyface smiled as he inspected the

fetuses. There were dozens sloshing around in the jar. How perfect, he thought as he unscrewed the lid of the jar and laughed as he dumped the fetuses into a large glowing blue vat labeled "Stem Cell Research".

CHAPTER 7

1

Irma Paddick was drunk and snored on the couch next to an empty bottle of bourbon while a game show blared on television, when Molly pulled her car into the driveway. Molly opened the front door a crack, saw her mom was asleep, and waved for Holtie to follow her inside.

"Keep quiet. Let's go upstairs," said Molly, as she snuck Holtie up to her room.

"We can hang out here for a while," said Molly as she sat down on the bed.

"Thanks for hiding me, Molly."

"It's nothing."

"I'm so sorry about Autumn," Holtie said and joined Molly on the bed.

"Holtie, I don't know if she meant to kill herself, but I think it might have been a Dopiod overdose."

"The biker we saw overdose last night, he was on Dopiods."

"Is he okay? That was scary."

"No. Overdosed and died."

"I'm scared, Holtie," said Molly. She scooted over and hugged him.

"Me too, Molly," said Holtie as he held her tight in his muscular arms.

Molly gazed into Holtie's eyes as an intense passion welled up inside her. Holtie leaned in and gently kissed her on the lips. The warmth of his body against hers made her feel safe, and she never wanted the moment to end. Holtie caressed the hair out of her face and leaned back on the bed. Molly grabbed his crotch, undid his pants, and started giving him a sloppy blowjob.

2

Karen pulled up outside the old abandoned industrial building. The sign on the fence had been spray painted with a large back frowny face symbol. She studied the frowny face symbol on the pill bottles she had found in her Holtie's bedroom and felt this simply couldn't be a coincidence.

Karen found the gates unchained and ajar. She made her way to the building, opened the big creaky double doors, and went inside.

"Hello? Is anybody here?" Karen called into the dark hallway.

She heard sounds coming from somewhere deep within the building. A bubbling. Liquid of some sort. She slowly walked along the corridor, hands feeling the walls to guide her as her eyes darted in all directions. She turned a corner and saw a door that glowed with a green light that radiated from around the threshold.

"Hello? My name is Karen and I'd like to speak to a manager," said Karen. She reached for the knob and threw the glowing door open.

"Hello," said Doctor Frownyface. "I'm the manager."

Doctor Frownyface and Missy Gore stood in the doorway of the laboratory, flanked by the Serial Abortionists in hazmat suits. Karen let out a yelp.

"I found these Dopiods in my son's room," explained Karen. "And I just wanted to see…"

"Why you've already seen too much. And that was a bad move, Karen," smirked Doctor Frownyface. "Seize her!"

Karen struggled as the Serial Abortionists grabbed her by the arms and dragged her into Frownyface's lab.

"What's happening? What is this place? Who are you people?" Karen yelled.

"My name is Doctor Frownyface. And you're in the wrong place at the wrong time," said Doctor Frownyface.

"What are you doing to me?" Karen cried, as the Serial Abortionists held her before the giggling Doctor Frownyface.

"You're going to help me test a new vaccine to protect against a super-virus," said Doctor Frownyface, as Missy Gore handed him a glowing green spray bottle.

"But I don't have a super-virus," gasped Karen.

Doctor Frownyface grinned and misted Karen's face with the spray bottle.

"You do now," he said with a smile.

"No! No! Not a super-virus! Nooooo!" screamed Karen.

"Smells like old books and e-readers," said Doctor Frownyface.

The Serial Abortionists held Karen tightly as she thrashed around, gurgled, convulsed, and vomited. Karen collapsed to her knees, sneezed, and then farted.

3

Holtie fucked the shit out of Molly as she lay prone on the bed. He pulled her hair, slapped her ass, and drove his dick hard between her legs. The head of his penis rubbed firmly against her G-spot. Holtie abruptly pulled out of Molly. She rolled over on her back and spread her legs for missionary. She grabbed Holtie by the collar and kissed him deeply, while his giant cock slid in and out of her pussy.

"Oh fuck! Oh fuck! Oh shit!" Molly gasped.

Holtie put his hand over her mouth to cover her moans. Molly dug her nails into Holtie's back and her legs began to quiver and shake uncontrollably as he screwed her to orgasm. Her legs tightened around Holtie's waist and she held her breath as she squirted and came all over his fat schlong.

Molly lit a joint and smiled while Holtie continued to plow her. She smoked and shuddered with ecstasy as Holtie's cock began to throb inside her.

"Yes! Cum in me, daddy," cooed Molly.

"You are so wet, baby. Fuck yes!" grunted Holtie as he spurted cum inside of Molly. "Oh my god! Oh my god! Oh my god!"

4

"Oh my god! Oh my god! Oh my god! What is happening to me?" Karen sputtered as she laid on the ground and gasped for air. Mucus poured from Karen's nose and mouth. She sneezed, puked, and farted again.

"I think we've done it!" said Doctor Frownyface to Missy Gore. "The effects of this generation of super-virus are strong. The people are addicted and hungry for their Dopiod fix, and this viral variant will be perfect for my new and improved… super-virus laden Dopiods!"

"You won't get away with this, Frownyface!" Karen moaned.

"I think I might," cackled Doctor Frownyface as he handed Missy Gore a glowing blue syringe. "Here, test out the new vaccine."

Missy Gore moved towards Karen and held the syringe of luminescent blue fluid in front of Karen's vomit-covered face.

"Missy Gore! Stop playing with Mrs. Thump and test the vaccine," Doctor Frownyface ordered. "This super-virus grows more and more contagious by the hour and deadlier with each new mutation. We have no time to waste."

Missy Gore took the syringe away from Karen's face and injected it into her own arm. Doctor Frownyface picked up another glowing blue syringe, stabbed it into his shoulder, and pushed down the plunger.

"Ah, refreshing," said Doctor Frownyface.

"What about me?" stammered Karen. "Give me the vaccine!"

Doctor Frownyface menacingly walked to where Karen lay sick and hulked over her.

"No," said Doctor Frownyface, booping Karen's nose.

Karen farted, moaned, and struggled to stay conscious. Doctor Frownyface chortled and moved to the door.

"What do we do with this mess?" asked Missy Gore in her thick Russian accent.

"Let the Serial Abortionists take care of her," Doctor Frownyface said as a big smile cracked his face. The Serial Abortionists in their hazmat suits advanced on the weeping Karen with their vacuums. The sound of vacuuming, screaming, and farting filled the air.

5

Molly laid next to Holtie on the bed. She now wore only his t-shirt. Holtie took a puff on the joint and sighed. Molly felt the hot cum slip down her thighs as it dripped out of her pussy.

"I think I hear something downstairs. My mom must be awake for a refill," said Molly. "Holtie, I want you to promise me you won't try Dopiods."

Molly climbed on top of Holtie and took off his t-shirt. Holtie passed Molly the joint. She took a hit and her breasts heaved on the inhale. Her smooth labia rubbed and embraced the shaft of his penis as his dick head rubbed against her clit.

"Herb is safer than Dopiods," Holtie said, getting hard. "And weed is more my speed anyway."

"Good," said Molly as she began to grind into Holtie. "Let's go again. I want you to cum in my ass."

Molly set down the joint, picked up a dildo, and started making out with Holtie.

6

Downstairs, Irma Paddick filled a glass with ice and opened a kitchen cupboard looking for booze. She tried the fridge. She tried the freezer. She looked all over the kitchen for another bottle of bourbon and found nothing.

"Where's my bourbon?" Irma burped.

Irma bent down to check a lower cabinet. Nothing. Maybe it got pushed to the back of the cabinet, she thought, and leaned way down. Something in her back went click and then pop.

"Ow. My fucking back," groaned Irma.

7

Mayor Stu Paddick stood behind a podium outside City Hall and smoked a big cigar. He wore a sequin Uncle Sam Hat, American flag sunglasses, and an "I'm the MAYOR, bitch!" t-shirt. His aides wore sparkly patriotic American flag outfits and held sparklers. A small crowd had assembled in front of the podium to listen to the mayor's speech.

"I ordered a crackdown on marijuana addicts and it's working. Why? Because I'm the MAYOR, bitch!" Paddick boasted into the microphone, to the genial applause of the audience. "An incredible response, so far! These thugs can get right the fuck out of my town! Am I right? Thank you. I love you!"

A crowd of young protesters marched down the sidewalk. They carried "Ban Dopiods" and "Leave Our Weed Alone!" signs and chanted over the mayor's speech.

"One, two, three, four! We don't want Dopiods anymore! Five, six, seven, eight! Smoking weed is really great!"

"Oh, yeah?" yelled the mayor. "What's the root of

all of our problems? Marijuana is! Marijuana causes school shootings, homelessness, bad credit, elder abuse, car warranty scams! And do you know how many trashy pulp novels have been written on marijuana?"

"Booo!" hissed the crowd of protesters.

"Marijuana is the gateway drug to Dopiods. Taking a pill is safer than smoking marijuana, right?" said the mayor, taking a big puff on his cigar. "And everyone knows smoking is bad for you!"

"Boo! Boo! Booooo!!!" booed the protesters.

The mayor looked indignant as the protesters threw eggs, heads of lettuce, and a few rotten tomatoes at him. The mayor's aides stepped back with their sparklers as rotten produce rained down on Stu Paddick.

VOTE!
I'M THE MAYOR, BITCH!
STU ★ ★ ★ PADDICK

8

Irma Paddick held a bag of bourbon bottles as she waddled out of the liquor store. Harley Auspuffrohr stood outside the store as he sold Dopiods to passersby and watched Irma as she clutched her aching back.

"Hey, lady," whispered Harley.

"What do you want?" croaked Irma.

"I couldn't help notice you have a sore back. I think I've got something that could help," said Harley as he held up a bottle of Dopiods for Irma to see.

"I don't have any more money," wheezed Irma.

"This bottle is on me," said Harley. "Just come back and see me when you need more."

Irma took the pill bottle from Harley, looked at the frowny face symbol on the bottle, and walked away holding her sore back.

9

Holtie grabbed the lube and squirted a little out on Molly's tight butthole as he thrusted his hot love piston in and out of her vagina from behind. He grabbed her butt and rubbed her asshole with his thumb. Then he pushed his thumb in, just a little bit. Molly moaned and arched her back. Holtie pulled his thumb out of Molly's sphincter, squirted on more lube, and went back to rubbing her hole with his thumb.

"That wasn't so bad, huh?" said Holtie as he pulled his penis out of her vagina.

"More lube," said Molly.

"Just relax your ass," Holtie said. "Don't squeeze your butthole. Push out. That relaxes it."

Holtie ran his fingers through the lube and inserted his middle finger into Molly's asshole.

"Ow! So full," moaned Molly. "Mmmmm."

Holtie slid his middle finger into Molly's ass up to his second knuckle and then pulled it out again.

"Give it just a second," cried Molly, wincing. "I need just a second."

"Relax. Relax," reassured Holtie, rubbing her hole again as he spanked her ass.

"Ouch," Molly said and let go a cry.

Holtie dripped a little more lube above Molly's rectum and let it glide down onto the two fingers he now slid into her butthole.

"Oh! Oh, yes! Fuck, yes!" Molly gasped, signaling to Holtie it was time to saddle up.

Holtie pressed his dick firmly against Molly's loosened asshole and pushed. The head of his cock slid in and then popped right back out. He mopped up the lube with his dickhead and used his hand to guide himself halfway into Molly's butt.

"Ugh! Fuck!" Molly cried. "Fuck! You are THICK!"

Holtie smiled and chuckled to himself as he pushed

his dick all the way inside Molly's asshole. She gasped again and he pulled out.

"Was that all the way?" asked Molly.

"Yes. Are you doing okay?"

"Mmm hmm," Molly said, biting her lip.

Molly wiggled her butt and gaped her asshole at Holtie. Holtie smacked her ass and she cried out. He mounted her and stuck his dick all the way in her ass.

"So big!" moaned Molly.

Holtie's erection pulsed and got harder. He fucked her slow at first and his mind zeroed in on the sensations of his meaty shaft as it slid against the walls of her ass.

"Yes. Fuck me. Fuck me, daddy," Molly cried. "Cum in my ass. I want your cum. Cum in my ass, daddy," Molly purred.

"Oh fuck," growled Holtie, thrusting his cock faster. "I'm about to cum. Let me cum on your face."

Molly jumped up and kneeled in front of Holtie. With her hands on his hips, she blew him furiously. Holtie pulled his dick from Molly's mouth and began to jerk off fast. Every muscle in his body tightened and he shot two thick ropes of pearly cum across Molly's sweet face.

Molly lapped at the cum as it dripped from Holtie's dick. Then she took Holtie's cock back into her mouth and sucked him some more. Holtie shook from the surprise, orgasmed again, and fell back on the bed. He pulled his boxers back on and looked around for his T-shirt.

"We should go hang out by the river, smoke some more weed and have a few beers," Molly said as Holtie's cum oozed down her face. "I just want to relax and spend time with you."

"I'd like that. But…"

"But what?"

"Only if you let me drive your car," chuckled Holtie.

"Deal!" Molly said as she put on her panties. "I'm going to go clean up."

Molly walked to the bathroom and admired her crazy sex hair in the mirror. Before she washed her face, she ran her finger through Holtie's cum, tasted a little and licked her lips.

10

Irma Paddick swerved down the street in her land yacht, nearly nicked a fire hydrant and almost flattened the neighbor's mailbox. She pulled into her driveway and grabbed the bag of bourbon from the floor of the car. She stumbled into the house and into the kitchen, where she refreshed her glass of ice and poured herself a big glass of liquor.

She regarded the Dopiod pill bottle with a look of suspicion for a moment. But what could it hurt, thought Irma. She popped the lid off the bottle and washed one of the tiny green pills down with a gulp of bourbon. She looked at the size of the remaining pills and shrugged. Free and small, take them all, thought Irma. She dumped a few more Dopiods directly into her glass of bourbon and stirred them around with her big fat sausage fingers.

Irma waddled to the couch with the pills and bourbon. She sat down with a thud, grabbed the remote and flicked on the television. Her eyes grew wide and her stomach began to gurgle.

※ ※ ※

Holtie put on his shoes and checked his text messages. He had one text from Harley that just said, *Where the hell are you?*

Molly entered the bedroom wearing fresh make-up and a bikini and slid into a pair of fresh shorts from her dresser drawer.

"I think I heard something downstairs again," said Holtie.

"It's definitely my mom. We'll just slip out the window," Molly said as she slid into a skin tight belly shirt.

Holtie gave Molly a kiss as he helped her out the window. They scampered across the roof and climbed down a vine covered trellis on the side of the house to Molly's car.

※ ※ ※

Irma stood rigid before the television, her arms and legs extended out to the sides like a starfish. Her eyes grew even bigger, then rolled up into the back of her head. She began to convulse and knocked over both the bottle of Dopiods and her bottle of bourbon.

Yellow foam poured from Irma's mouth as she gasped for air and clutched at her throat. She whipped around and collapsed into a puddle of bourbon on the pill strewn floor. Her head hit the ground next to her bottle of bourbon, and a glob of acid yellow foam rolled off her tongue.

Irma twitched, then she lay motionless.

11

A group of young protesters had shown up outside the liquor store with signs that read "Stop The Dopiod Crisis". Harley walked away from the store and talked on a flip phone.

"Hey, Frownyface, man. This is Harley from the Pen15 Gang. Hey, man, we're almost out of product," said Harley. "I'm wondering if you've got that new and improved batch of Dopiods ready? People are really itchy for this shit, you know what I mean? People can't get enough."

Doctor Frownyface talked on a giant old brick cell phone while the Serial Abortionists vacuumed and Karen moaned in the next room. Missy Gore sat across from him and filled the pill bottles labeled with the frowny face symbol with fresh Dopiods.

"Good news! You're in luck," crowed Doctor

Frownyface. "I've just made a new batch of Dopiods that packs a little bit more of… a kick."

Karen gurgled and screamed over the sound of the vacuums. Frownyface giggled and Missy Gore paused to savor the sound of the screams that reverberated through the lab. They both smiled.

"Meet me at the river this evening. Near the town's water reservoir intake drain," said Doctor Frownyface. "That's right. We can make a deal then. Ta-ta!"

Harley snapped the flip phone shut and hopped on his bike.

"Ta-ta. Ta-ta. Who the fuck says ta-ta?" snapped Harley as he shook his head and fired up his bike. "This guy is a total fucking weirdo."

Harley roared up the road to the junkyard to retrieve the rest of the Pen15 Gang.

CHAPTER 8

1

"There's Muffy," said Molly.

Holtie pulled the car into the lot by the river. Muffy wore only a skimpy bikini and sunglasses as she bought beer from Jimmy the Beer Guy. She waved Molly and Holtie over to join her. What remained of the squad were spread out on towels on the beach as they sunbathed, smoked, and drank.

"Hey, guys," said Muffy. "Wait? You're wearing something else from earlier. Were you two just fucking without me? Oooh, lovebirds."

"Muffy, please. I never kiss and tell," said Molly. "Hand me one of those beers."

Poppers jumped up and bounced over to Molly with a beer.

"I'm Poppers!" said Poppers.

"Hey, I'll go get our stuff out of the trunk," said Holtie as he started walking back to the car.

The Pen15 Gang rumbled down the road on their motorcycles. Harley spotted Holtie as he walked to Molly's car and signaled for the rest of the gang to follow him into the parking lot.

"You!" yelled Harley as he rolled up to the side of Molly's car and killed his bike. "Holtie!"

"Hey, Harley," said Holtie.

"Hey, nothing. I didn't see where you went after that clothing store robbery, Holtie," Harley said as he stormed up to Holtie. "The guys here say you left your bike at the scene like a bonehead. And you left me and Nacho dealing with those Mall Ninjas. Alone!"

"I wasn't thinking, Harley," said Holtie. "How's Nacho?"

"Nacho's dead, man," Harley said and snapped his fingers. "Here."

The biker with the handlebar mustache tossed a small bag of Dopiod pill bottles to Harley. Harley shoved the bag into Holtie's chest.

"These are the last of that first batch of Dopiods," Harley said angrily to Holtie. "The guys and I have to go to the town's reservoir to pick up our next shipment. Push these pills on the river today."

"Okay, sure, Harley. I'm on it. Whatever you say, man," said Holtie.

"It is whatever I say, man. You're in the Pen15 now and as the leader of the Pen15, when I say we're committing crimes and such, we do whatever fucking I say."

"I understand," Holtie said. "But these Dopiods are killing people, Harley."

"Did I ask you?" shrieked Harley.

"No, Harley," said Holtie.

"Listen, Holtie. You're either in the Pen15 Gang or you're out of the Pen15 Gang," Harley snarled, pulled out a switchblade and waved it in front of Holtie's nose. "And there's only one way out of the Pen15, do I make myself clear?

"Perfectly clear," Holtie gulped as he eyeballed Harley's knife.

"Sell the Dopiods. The cops are only messing with kids when they smell reefer," Harley said. "Dopiods don't smell like reefer. It's not rocket science, dingus. Sell the Dopiods and bring me all the money! You work for me! That's what you do now!"

Harley hopped on his bike and pointed at Holtie menacingly. Then Harley and the Pen15 Gang roared away toward the town's water reservoir and left Holtie in the dust. Holtie gathered his and Molly's stuff, looked at the Dopiod pill bottles, shook his head in concern, and shut the trunk.

2

Mayor Paddick came home to change clothes. The smell of moldy vegetables and rotten eggs followed him like a cloud.

"Honey, I'm home! I got egged by some protester

thugs at my campaign rally," said the mayor. "I figured since I had to run home and change, maybe we could have some sex."

Irma Paddick lay unresponsive on the pill covered floor, next to the empty bottle of bourbon. Stu had been here with Irma before, but he never knew how to proceed.

"Maybe just a quickie?" said the mayor.

He looked at Irma for a moment and considered the mechanics of having sex with her lifeless body. He threw out his shoulder just rolling her over the last time this had happened.

"Ah, just like on our wedding night," the mayor said and decided against sex with his wife. "Nah, not worth it."

Stu Paddick headed upstairs to change clothes.

3

Karen Thump sat alone in a room, an old soap factory office, tied to a chair. Covered in sweat and vomit, she looked around groggily and tried to make sense of her surroundings.

"You're sick, Frownyface!" she spat.

"I'm not sick," chuckled Doctor Frownyface. "I'm vaccinated."

Missy Gore handed Doctor Frownyface a wrench. The mad doctor tinkered with a device, making more adjustments on some sort of mysterious ray gun.

"No, Karen, you're the only one sick here," said Doctor Frownyface over his shoulder as he poured a handful of emeralds into a chamber on the device and shut the lid. "But if you want to see really sick then you should check out what I'm about to do with my latest invention… the enlargement ray!"

Karen gurgled and sputtered in the other room as Doctor Frownyface placed a petri dish of green gel under the ray gun. Missy Gore put on her googles. Doctor Frownyface put another pair of goggles over his other googles.

"Full power, Missy Gore!" yelled Doctor Frownyface.

Missy Gore flipped several switches, and the enlargement ray began to light up and smoke.

"Activating enlargement ray!" cackled Doctor Frownyface.

He grabbed a large switch, turned to watch, and then threw the switch. There was a blinding flash of light. The petri dish began to stretch and grow to an incredible size. Inside the gigantic petri dish, huge viruses wriggled and jiggled. Doctor Frownyface smiled big and threw the switch back, deactivating the machine. Frownyface took off his extra pair of goggles and laughed.

"It worked!" screamed Doctor Frownyface. "I have created a new form of super-virus! You two…"

Doctor Frownyface pointed at the Serial Abortionists and they snapped to attention. The doctor began to back slowly towards the office where Karen sputtered.

"…pick up my SUPER super-viruses!" Doctor Frownyface said, gritting his teeth.

The Serial Abortionists shuffled to the giant petri dish. As Serial Abortionist Frank picked up one of the undulating orbs, his eyes turned black. He shook violently, farted, and then projectile vomited all over Serial Abortionist Joe. Covered in his uncle's vomit, Serial Abortionist Joe's eyes also turned black. He too farted and projectile vomited. The Serial Abortionists shit themselves, their mouths filled with a blood red froth, and then they fell to the ground motionless.

Doctor Frownyface laughed. He turned to stare at Karen and grinned from ear to ear. Karen screamed.

"The test was a success," said Doctor Frownyface. "My new super super-virus is more powerful than I ever could have imagined."

Karen whimpered. Doctor Frownyface looked over his shoulder and got serious.

"I'm famished," Doctor Frownyface said to Missy Gore. "Would you like to split a salad kit with me?"

Missy Gore shrugged and headed out of the room. Doctor Frownyface followed.

"I really just like the croutons and cheese. But a whole salad kit is always too much for me," said Doctor Frownyface. "And it's never good later when you try to eat it because the lettuce gets soggy."

Doctor Frownyface waved goodbye to Karen. And left the room. Karen tried to lift her head, but she now felt so weak. Karen looked from the motionless bodies of the Serial Abortionists to an old telephone sitting on a desk in the office.

4

Holtie finished a Dopiod transaction with a few river bums, then walked back to his towel by the girls. His cellphone rang, but he didn't recognize the number.

"Holtie!" whispered the voice of Karen on the other end.

"Hey, Ma," said Holtie.

"Holtie! Holtie!" gasped Karen. "I'm being held captive by some kind of mad scientist in the old industrial building."

"Ma! What? Old industrial building?" Holtie said in a panic. "I'm coming to save you, Ma!"

Karen was still tied to the chair. She had knocked the receiver off the phone in Doctor Frownyface's office and dialed Holtie with her nose. She leaned into the phone and sobbed.

"His name is Doctor Frownyface. He's making some kind of super-virus!" cried Karen. "And he's putting it in these pills, Holtie. The Dopiods!"

A rubber-gloved hand reached in from behind Karen and hung up the receiver on the phone. Doctor Frownyface had returned.

"No! Holtie, help!" screamed Karen. "No!"

"I'm afraid visiting hours are over," said Doctor Frownyface.

"My son is coming to save me!" said Karen

"My dear, nothing can save you now," laughed Doctor Frownyface. "You see, my Serial Abortionists have been terminally infected with my super super-viruses. They're super super-spreaders, Karen."

"What do you mean, you mad man?!" yelled Karen.

"What I mean is that you most certainly have been infected with my super super-virus and soon you'll be a super super-spreader."

"No," gasped Karen. "No!"

"And now you've lured your son into my lab. And soon he'll be infected with my super super-virus, and he'll be dead and be a super super-spreader. And so on and so on…"

"No, not Holtie!" wept Karen.

"Yes. And the only way to stop my super-virus will be through me," Doctor Frownyface said with a grin. "For I, Doctor Frownyface, will be the only one with the super-vaccine!"

Missy Gore entered the lab eating a salad- minus the croutons and cheese.

5

Molly, Muffy, and the other girls sat around Holtie in their bikinis and looked scared. Holtie hit redial in a panic and stared at his phone.

"The line is dead," said Holtie.

"What's happening?" asked Muffy.

"Some lunatic is holding my mom hostage in the old industrial building," said Holtie.

"Should we call the police?" asked Muffy.

"No police!" said Molly. "The cops might be looking for Holtie."

"What did you do?" Muffy asked Holtie.

"It's a long story," said Holtie.

"He ran into some Mall Ninjas," Molly said.

"I'm so sorry," said Muffy, sympathetically.

The rest of the girls looked shocked and their hands went to their mouths upon hearing the news.

"I'll call my step-dad. He's the mayor," said Molly. "He'll know what to do."

Molly pulled out her phone and dialed Stu.

"Molly, I need to go!" said Holtie.

"It's my car!" Molly interjected. "I'm coming with you."

Holtie ran to the car. Molly, wearing only her bikini, followed behind, still on her phone, waiting for her step-dad to pick up. They jumped in the car, and Holtie backed out without looking and nearly hit Jimmy the Beer Guy.

"Hey! Watch where you're going!" yelled Jimmy the Beer Guy.

Holtie popped the car into gear and tore out of the parking lot in a cloud of dust.

6

Mayor Stu Paddick parked his car in a handicap spot and walked down the sidewalk. He had changed into a fresh "I'm the MAYOR, bitch!" t-shirt and wore a dark blazer and sunglasses. Several anti-Dopiod protesters stood in the middle of the sidewalk with "Stop Dopiods" signs.

The mayor stopped outside a massage parlor, when his phone rang. It was Molly. He rolled his eyes, shook his head, ignored the call and sent it to voicemail. Stu hadn't got sex at home and still felt horny. He put the phone back in his pocket, looked around to see if anyone was watching, and stepped inside the massage parlor.

7

Karen was still tied to the chair when Doctor Frownyface dragged her into his laboratory. He positioned her between the Serial Abortionists and the enlarged petri dish full of giant pulsating super-viruses.

"Once my super-virus spreads, I'll sell people masks and hand sanitizers. And the toilet paper! You won't even believe what I'll be able to charge for that," continued Doctor Frownyface. "People will pay me for them. And all that, my dear, will be followed by my newly developed super-vaccine."

"You monster," gasped Karen.

"But it won't stop there. No," chuckled Doctor Frownyface; "then there will be lamination machines to laminate vaccine cards, vaccine passport apps, and super-virus dead memorials to sculpt. And I, Doctor Frownyface, will be there first. The only supplier of salvation to the simpering citizenry seeking to survive my super-virus!"

Doctor Frownyface wiped the spittle from his lips and beard. A giant grin spread across his face.

"Help! Let me go! Help!" screamed Karen.

"And the people will sing praises to my name and I will be beloved," smiled Doctor Frownyface. "The architect of an unstoppable legacy, remembered as the greatest scientist in history. Doctor Frownyface! The man who stopped the super-virus!"

Missy Gore entered the laboratory with a briefcase and filled it with glowing blue super-vaccine syringes.

"You fiend," wheezed Karen.

"But stopping a super-virus will cost a pretty penny, you see," Doctor Frownyface persisted with his monologue and ignored Karen. "And I will be there to rake in the pennies. Missy Gore!"

Missy Gore closed the briefcase full of super-vaccines, grabbed the enlargement ray and headed for the door.

"We must make our escape. Careful with the enlargement ray, Missy Gore. It might be useful later," Doctor Frownyface said as he turned back to Karen. "I'm sure you understand that we can't take you with us and risk you getting sick in the car."

"I just had it detailed," Missy Gore said, in her thick Russian accent, and exited the laboratory. Doctor Frownyface followed her.

"No! No!" screamed Karen. "Release me!"

"Farewell. We're off to the river to unleash the super-virus into the town reservoir," giggled Doctor Frownyface, "spreading my super-virus first upon the foolish masses of this city, and then upon the world!"

Missy Gore sat in the driver seat of a large tanker truck as Doctor Frownyface ran from the building. He jumped in the passenger seat and Missy Gore floored it. The truck rumbled away right as Holtie and Molly arrived at the old industrial building.

Holtie jumped out of the car and started to chase after the tanker truck, before he realized he couldn't catch it. He doubled back and ran into the building to save Karen, followed by Molly in her tiny bikini.

Holtie and Molly ran down the corridor toward where they could hear Karen's screams. They burst into Doctor Frownyface's temporary laboratory and found Karen groaning, tied to a chair.

"Holtie!" cried Karen.

"Ma!" screamed Holtie.

"Holtie, don't come any closer!" sputtered his mother. Holtie and Molly froze in their tracks, well away from Karen.

"Ma!" yelled Holtie in despair.

"Holtie, I've been infected with a deadly and contagious super-virus and have little time left to explain," cried Karen. "He's created a super-virus!"

"Who, Ma?" said Holtie.

"Doctor Frownyface. He's going to the river, to the town's water reservoir, to contaminate the town's water supply with the super-virus," said Karen. "Listen, Holtie. The only way to stop the super-virus is with the super-vaccine."

"Where's the super-vaccine, Ma?" asked Holtie.

"He took most of it with him," said Karen. "But they may have left some super-vaccines behind."

"Where, Ma?" asked Holtie.

"In the desk," cried Karen as she indicated the desk where Missy Gore had taken the syringes.

"Where?" said Molly as she examined the desk.

"Who is this, Holtie?" Karen said sternly. "Is this the girl you've been fornicating with in your bedroom?"

"Ma!" yelled Holtie.

"I think I found two super-vaccines," said Molly as she pulled two glowing blue syringes from a desk drawer.

"You take one, Molly," Holtie said as he seized one of the needles. "I'll give the other one to my mom!"

"No!" yelled Karen. "It's too late for me. I love you, Holtie. Take the super-vaccines. Take them. Take them now!"

Karen began to lurch and writhe on the chair. Holtie and Molly injected themselves in their shoulders with the super-vaccine syringes. Karen's eyes turned black, and she projectile-vomited all over herself and diarrhea shot from beneath her perfectly pleated skirt.

"No! Ma!" Holtie cried in terror. "Noooooo!!!"

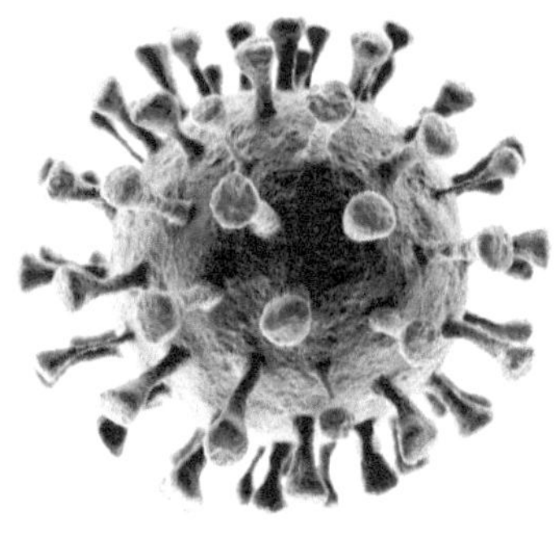

8

Mayor Paddick stood by the massage table as he listened to Molly's voicemail on his phone. He wore only a towel, his jacket and clothes on a chair.

"Stupid teenagers," snorted Stu. "What is going on with this girl now?"

The mayor set his phone down on the massage table as the massage girl entered. Goo Dong wore silk shorts and a short silk robe. The mayor laid down on his back on the massage table and adjusted his towel.

"Ready for massage, big boy?" asked Goo Dong.

"Who's got two thumbs and likes to point with a different appendage?" asked Stu. His erection bounced under the towel and pointed to his face. "This guy! Hey, Goo Dong? Do you mind taking care of that for me?"

"You pay me extra," Goo Dong said and slapped the mayor's hard-on beneath the towel.

The mayor picked up his phone off the massage table and dialed the number Doctor Frownyface had given him.

"Fine. Whatever. Reach into my jacket pocket," said the mayor, "there is an envelope labelled "hush money" or some shit. Help yourself to a few bills, cuz I'm the MAYOR, bitch!"

Goo Dong began to jerk Paddick off under the towel.

"Hey, Frownyface! It's the mayor," said Stu into his phone. "I'm starting to catch a lot of flack from the public for your Dopiods. Now, my step-daughter just called me in a panic saying something was up in the old industrial building. Whoa."

The mayor's eyes rolled into the back of his head as Goo Dong stroked his dick faster. Doctor Frownyface was in the passenger seat of the large tanker truck and talked on his old brick cell phone.

"I'm sure it is nothing to concern yourself with," said Doctor Frownyface.

"Oh yeah," said Stu.

"Kids these days, am I right?" Doctor Frownyface said with a nervous laugh.

"Slower," said the mayor.

"Kids. These. Days. Am. I. Right?" Said Doctor Frownyface slowly and deliberately.

"Slower, slower," said the mayor, making orgasmic faces as Good Dong rapidly beat his meat faster and faster. Stu snapped back to the phone call. "No, not you, Frownyface. I'm out on official mayor's business. So anyway, I don't think I can allow Dopiods much longer."

"I see," said Doctor Frownyface.

"Yeah, too many people are overdosing and now the press is going up my ass asking too many questions," said the mayor.

"Going up your ass is extra," said Goo Dong.

"No, not you, Goo Dong," said the mayor, but nodding to let her know he would, in fact, pay extra.

"So anyway, I don't know what to tell you, Frownyface. The press is calling it a Dopiod crisis. The public wants me to do something. I'm probably going to have to come out against Dopiods eventually. So, um, what do you expect me to do? Hello? Hello, Frownyface? Are you there?"

The mayor looked at his phone. The line was dead. The door of the massage room was kicked open and Doctor Frownyface entered the room. Missy Gore stood behind him. She held a tranquilizer gun. Goo Dong screamed. The Mayor panicked and flipped over onto his stomach.

"I expect you to enjoy a taste of your own medicine," laughed Doctor Frownyface.

"Frownyface?" said Mayor Paddick in confusion. "What?"

Missy Gore stepped forward, raised the tranquilizer gun and took aim at the mayor.

"Spa shooter!" yelled Goo Dong.

"Wait! Frownyface! No!" the terrified mayor screamed.

Missy Gore fired the tranquilizer gun and launched a dart full of glowing green fluid directly into Stu Paddick's ass. The mayor let out a blood-curdling scream and his eyes turned black as he convulsed naked on the massage table. Stu projectile vomited all over the wall and a stream of putrid diarrhea shot from beneath his towel.

Doctor Frownyface laughed as the mayor lay still

on the massage table. Goo Dong's eyes turned black and she began to writhe as diarrhea shot from her skimpy silk shorts. Goo Dong turned, projectile vomited all over the motionless mayor, and collapsed on top of him.

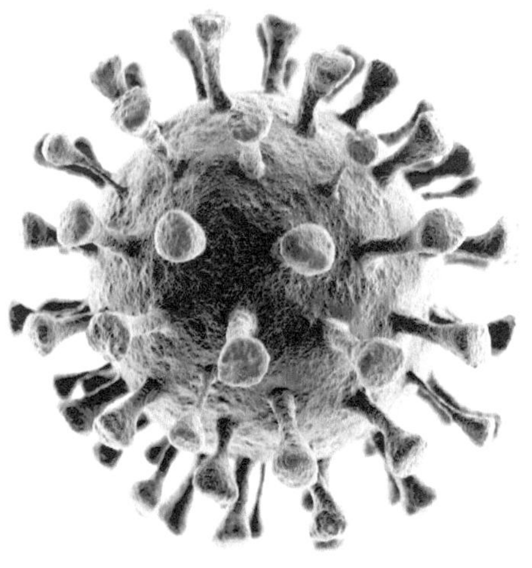

CHAPTER 9

1

Holtie was focused on driving as he raced through the streets. His right hand was on the gear shift. Molly placed her hand on his and noticed his still fresh Pen15 tattoo.

"Holtie? Why did you want to join the Pen15 Gang?" Molly asked.

"My uncle was Pen15. One of the originals. He and his buddies grew up on Pennsylvania and 15th street, hence the name. He was the fastest, baddest biker in town. He was on top of the world, and then…" Holtie explained as his voice cracked, "and then… fucking river sharks, man."

Holtie hit the steering wheel with the palm of his hand. Molly's hand went to her mouth.

"I'm so sorry," she said.

"I must have seen him jump sharks in that river hundreds of times solo," Holtie said. "But he got cocky. Took his old lady with him in a sidecar. In the heat of river shark mating season. While she was on her period."

"Wow, that's just so… relatable," Molly said. "But why do they spell it like that? You must know what it looks like."

"It looks like I'm a fucking badass!" said Holtie.

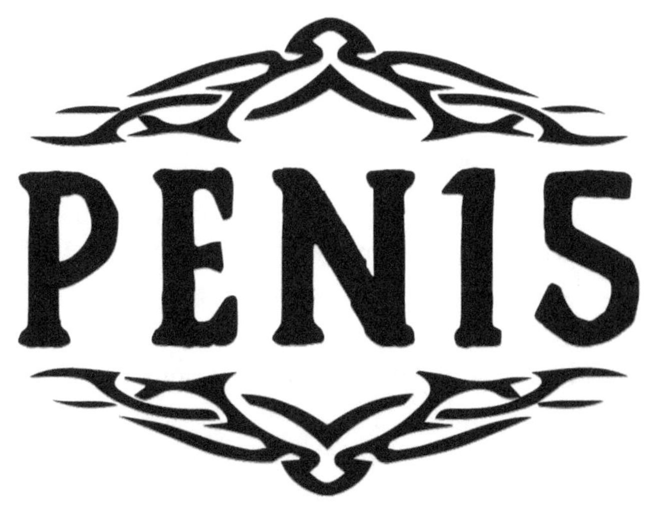

2

Missy Gore drove the tanker truck up to the town's water reservoir. Doctor Frownyface got out and moved toward the truck's cargo release mechanism, as Holtie and Molly arrived in Molly's car and screeched to a stop. Holtie grabbed the Mall Ninja sword out of the back seat of the car and ran towards the tanker truck. Molly, in her bikini, chased after him.

"How can this be? How did they survive my

super-virus?" growled Doctor Frownyface as he hurriedly flipped switches on the tanker truck. "Missy Gore, we must hurry and release the super-virus into the town's water supply!"

"Don't make a move, Frownyface," yelled Holtie.

"This is impossible!" cried Doctor Frownyface.

"Where did you get the sword?" Missy Gore asked Holtie.

"Mall Ninjas," Holtie said coldly.

Doctor Frownyface and Missy Gore reacted with shock at the news and their hands went to their mouths.

"I'm so sorry," said Missy Gore, in her thick Russian accent.

Holtie gripped the sword in front of him. Doctor Frownyface snarled at Holtie and Molly. Harley and the remaining Pen15 Gang stepped out of the shadows and approached the tanker truck.

"We're here, Frownyface," said Harley. "Where are the Dopiods?"

"I'm a little busy," said Doctor Frownyface as he fiddled and flicked more switches in the tanker truck cargo release. "I'll get them in just a moment."

"There aren't going to be any more Dopiods! You hear me?" yelled Holtie.

"Excuse me?" roared Harley, incensed. "What did you just say?"

Harley pulled out his gun and pointed it at Holtie and Molly. Holtie held the Mall Ninja sword and looked back and forth from Harley and the Pen15 Gang to Doctor Frownyface and Missy Gore.

"Holtie, Holtie, Holtie. Your behavior does not please me," said Harley angrily. "Get him, boys! And grab the girl, too."

The Pen15 Gang closed in on Holtie and Molly. Doctor Frownyface laughed as he finally flipped the switch that released the cargo hold of the tanker truck. The back of the truck opened, glowing green, and the giant super super-viruses spilled out towards the water reservoir. Holtie and Molly ran to the tanker truck.

"You're finished, Frownyface!" yelled Holtie.

"I don't think I am," Doctor Frownyface rumbled through gritted teeth.

Giant super super-viruses flew from the back of the tanker truck and struck several of the Pen15 bikers. Doctor Frownyface laughed and clung to the truck's cargo release lever. Holtie saw his chance.

Holtie raised the Mall Ninja sword high above his head and swung as hard as he could towards Doctor Frownyface's left arm. Blood sprayed from the mad doctor's stump. Fresh blood rivered down Doctor Frownyface's lab coat and sprayed against the side of the tanker truck as he reeled backwards.

"My arm!" cried Doctor Frownyface. "I will destroy you!"

Holtie wildly waved the Mall Ninja sword and turned his attention to the Pen15 Gang as they surrounded him. Molly ran to the tanker truck's cargo release and flipped the switch back. The rear of the truck began to close, shutting out the green glow. Gigantic super super-viruses pounded against the cargo door as it slammed shut. Missy Gore pounced on Molly from behind.

"Why won't you die!" hissed Missy Gore with her ice cold Russian accent.

"Test me, bitch!" yelled Molly.

Missy Gore pulled a glowing green needle from her lab coat and tried to stab Molly with it. Molly hit Missy Gore's arm, and the syringe flew out of her hand and into the dirt beneath the tanker truck.

Molly lashed out at Missy Gore, clawed at her, and tore her clothes and lab coat. Missy gore slammed Molly against the blood soaked side of the truck and knocked her out. Molly fell to the ground unconscious. Missy Gore ran to attend to Doctor Frownyface's severed arm.

The Pen15 biker with the handlebar mustache and the biker with the scruffy beard came from behind Holtie and grabbed his arms. The biker with the handlebar mustache took Holtie's Mall Ninja sword and threw it away into some bushes, where it stuck point down in the dirt. Holtie struggled to break free.

"Let go of me!" screamed Holtie.

And they did. The two bikers began to thrash and convulse, and lost their grip on Holtie. Molly regained consciousness and Holtie ran over to help her.

Holtie dragged Molly away from the tanker truck

as the scruffy bearded biker and the biker with the handlebar mustache's eyes turned black and they puked all over each other and shit themselves to death. Harley looked horrified as more of the Pen15 bikers' eyes started to turn black, and he watched as they convulsed, vomited, shit themselves, and fell lifeless to the ground.

"What the fuck is this, Frownyface?!" screamed Harley.

Harley raised his gun as he walked toward Doctor Frownyface, who used the truck's bumper as leverage to pull himself upright. Doctor Frownyface quickly reached for the cargo release and grabbed the switch with his remaining rubber-gloved fist.

"Why don't you see for yourself?" Doctor Frownyface tittered.

Doctor Frownyface threw the lever and the back of the tanker truck opened again. The green glow returned and the giant super super-viruses spilled out toward the river.

"Are you okay?" Holtie asked Molly as they pulled themselves to safety.

"I think so," Molly said.

A giant super super-viruses sailed from the tanker truck, smacked Harley directly in the face and knocked him to the ground. Harley's gun flew out of his hand and skittered just out of reach. Harley groaned.

Missy Gore ripped a strip of cloth from her lab coat and tried to tie off Doctor Frownyface's bloody arm stump, but the doctor roughly pushed her away and pointed to the truck cab with his remaining hand.

"Grab the super-vaccines!" Doctor Frownyface commanded.

Holtie grabbed Molly's hand and they dodged the giant super super-viruses as they ran towards Molly's car. Harley crawled weakly to where his gun laid on the ground. Doctor Frownyface laughed as Harley's eyes turned black and he barfed all over the ground and his gun.

"You thought you could stop me?" Doctor Frownyface howled. "I am the arbiter of your doom! I am the bringer of pain and suffering! I am Doctor Frownyface!!!"

But Harley was not dead. As he crawled through a puddle of his own vomit, Harley stared up at Doctor Frownyface with wet black eyes. Harley picked up his gun with a weak and shaky arm and fired it three times toward Doctor Frownyface and the truck. One of the bullets missed entirely. One of the bullets struck the truck's fuel tank. The final bullet ricocheted off the bottom of the truck and sent sparks flying. The truck exploded in a fireball.

The force of the fiery blast threw Doctor Frownyface and Missy Gore high into the air and sent them sailing into the river amongst flaming debris. Harley collapsed in pool of his own puke. Holtie grabbed Molly and yanked her behind her car. Molly screamed and Holtie pulled her close to his chest.

Doctor Frownyface, motionless and bleeding, floated facedown in the river current. Missy Gore flailed, sputtered, and paddled through the water after him. A fin broke the surface of the water and a river shark followed them by the smell of the blood that poured from Doctor Frownyface's freshly amputated arm. Tornado sirens began to wail and police cars could be heard in the distance.

3

"I'm scared!" cried Molly. "What do we do?"

"Get in the car, Molly!" screamed Holtie. "We've got to get out of here! Now!"

Holtie and Molly jumped in Molly's car just as police lights illuminated the scene and the sound of sirens grew closer. Holtie fired the engine, hit the gas, and fishtailed out of the flaming truck wreckage beside the town's water reservoir. Molly cried and clung to Holtie as they sped away. Tornado sirens wailed and the radio played an emergency alert tone, followed by a special news report.

"We interrupt your regularly scheduled programming for this important news bulletin," said Newsman Wes Chestleydale, who sounded serious and panicked. "Reports are coming in that a deadly super-virus of untold danger is sweeping through the area. The Mayor is missing and presumed dead of the super-virus. Hazmat teams have surrounded the area.

The entire town is under quarantine until further notice."

Holtie and Molly sped away along the empty river road that headed out of town. Bomber planes flew overhead and the sound of bombs falling could be heard over the tornado sirens as the car careened into the distance. The last thing they saw of the town was the city limits sign, a white painted bicycle, and an American flag.

"The Governor has activated the National Guard to assist in fighting the super-virus menace. The President prepares to address the nation later this evening in response to the ongoing super-virus crisis," said Newsman Wes Chestleydale on the car radio. "Local businesses are hereby closed and citizens are ordered to stay in their homes and shelter in place until further notice. Stay vigilant, stay safe, and stay alive, Mr. and Mrs. America."

The airborne bomber planes retreated to a safe distance at top speed. Then the entire town disappeared in a flash of bright white light as an atomic blast destroyed everything in its wake. The town's fate had been sealed.

EPILOGUE

Molly and Holtie sat in the waiting room of an abortion clinic. It had been three months since they escaped their hometown. They made it as far as the coast and never once looked back. A nurse entered the waiting room.

"Molly Bellmead?" said the nurse.

"That's me," said Molly.

"The doctors will see you now," said the nurse in a thick Russian accent.

Missy Gore stood by the waiting room desk, disguised as a sexy nurse. The door to the abortion clinic office swung open and the Serial Abortionists stood inside with their vacuums. Missy Gore laughed. Molly and Holtie screamed.

* * *

The sun shined brightly on the tropical beach. The waitress carried a tray with a club sandwich and a piña colada on it to the deck chairs along the sand. She set the tray down on a table and reached into her apron for the check.

The ground shook. The palm trees swayed and screams erupted along the shore. The waitress looked up and her eyes grew huge. She screamed and ran away towards the parking lot as the tyrannosaurus burst out of the palm trees and ran after the tourists that dotted the beach.

A dodo bird scuttled across the sand and carefully tried to steal a nibble of the club sandwich on the tray. A thick rubber gloved hand reached out and shooed the bird away. The T-rex stomped menacingly toward a cabana and grabbed a colorful beach umbrella in its mighty jaws. Doctor Frownyface took a sip from his drink and laughed maniacally.

ACKNOWLEDGMENTS

This is the place I will thank everyone and acknowledge the gang of misfits that have contributed in significant ways to the Frownyverse. Specifically…

—My wife Janie for being super supportive when I came up with the character Doctor Frownyface in the summer of 2016 and first donned the costume. Many years later, when I showed her the outline for this story and explained how offensive it might be, she got what I was doing immediately and didn't leave me. I am grateful for her contributing little uncredited jokes and gags here and there, and for all the help she provided behind the scenes formatting and preparing this book for print. She is very patient with my creative endeavors and I love her.

—Shelea Van Hoose for being my editor, not judging me too harshly given what I just made her read, and for sparing me the embarrassment of bad writing. I mean, I know I write filthy crap, but at least now it's readable filthy crap that's been proofread.

—Dr. Brian King for his work on the Frownyface screenplay, all the creative feedback he's provided along the way, and the very unique stamp he put on the character of the Mayor. Yes, that is Dr. Brian King in the Uncle Sam hat. He has helped me on this project since it was only just a deck of scribbled note cards piled on a Las Vegas hotel room coffee table. Brian is a great friend and collaborator. I very much enjoy working with him and I don't think we've seen the last of Mayor Stu Paddick.

—Sarah Bollinger for striking a sexy pose in a hot pink bikini for the book cover. Which, I must admit, turned out way better than the bikini photo I had taken of myself. Definitely make sure to check her out online if you are over 18 years of age and have a major credit card.

—Jovanna Reyes for her bitchin' PEN15 Gang tattoo design. I can't wait for the first time someone comes up to me at a show and proudly displays her design permanently etched somewhere on their body. I don't advise it, mind you, but I look forward to it.

—My mother, who better not have gone against my advice and read this book. My sister, for being an awesome adventurer who, some would argue, is actually funnier than me. And lastly, my step-dad Monte, who we lost over 4th of July weekend this year. Well, we didn't exactly lose him. We know where he is. I mean we're not idiots. But in all seriousness, he died and my mom keeps his ashes in her house somewhere now. Somewhere. I don't know. Anyway, my point is sadness, etc.

Enough! The rest of you go without thanks. Be gone!!!

–Dusty Trice

ABOUT THE AUTHOR

Dusty Trice was born in Florence, AL, on December 14, 1981, and grew up in Bismarck, ND. He dreamed of being a writer and comedian ever since he was a little kid. He wrote humor columns for his high school student newspaper, won several student journalism awards for his political cartooning, and was the on-air host of Best of the Big Bands on Prairie Public Radio during the swing revival of the 1990s.

After high school, Dusty gave up on being funny and went to college at the University of Minnesota, where he floundered and was a terrible student, took on a massive amount of student loan debt, and ultimately was placed on academic probation. He eventually earned a B.S. in Political Science from North Dakota State University. B.S., as you know, is very important in politics.

Dusty was a political staffer for 15 years and worked on electoral campaigns and marijuana legalization. He also co-hosted a weekly political talk show on AM950 in the Twin Cities. As a beltway insider in Washington, D.C., Dusty eventually grew to hate politics and distrust all politicians. He decided to leave politics in 2012 to pursue his childhood dream of making people laugh with his jokes and not just his profession.

Dusty began moonlighting as a stand-up comedian in 2012 at the Comedy Zone in Charlotte, NC. He moved to Los Angeles in 2013 and co-created the Stand Up Bus in Hollywood in 2014. Dusty wrote and directed the short film MACARONI NECKLACES (2016), had a supporting role in SOME LIKE IT BORING (2018), and as the titular character in BEAUREGARD (2019), in which he did his own stunts… completely nude. He has since written several screenplays, pilot scripts and books, including RISE OF DOCTOR FROWNYFACE.

In his spare time, Dusty is an expert recreational gardener, tends to his fruit trees, and creates abstract art from tissue paper. Dusty Trice lives in Los Angeles with his wife Janie.

To learn more about Dusty Trice and join his mailing list, visit DustyTrice.com!

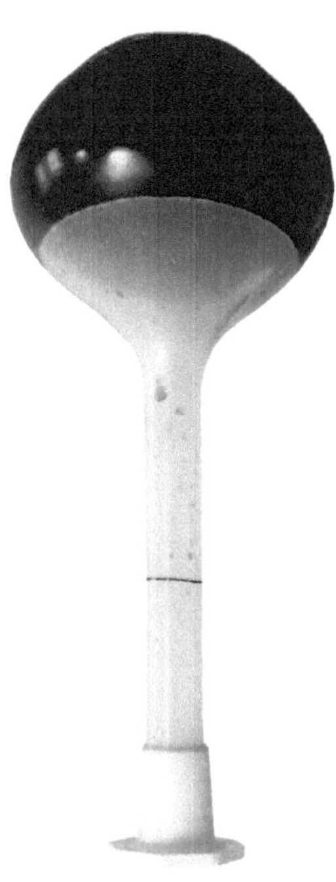

ALSO FROM READ-O-VISION

THEY'RE CHEAP!
THEY'RE PLASTIC!
THEY'RE SKELETONS!
AND THEY ARE HERE!

18+ DOCTOR FROWNYFACE PRESENTS
BONETINGLERS
CHEAP PLASTIC SKELETONS FROM HELL
DUSTY TRICE

AVAILABLE IN STORES NOW!